She patted th

Because she wa[...] do intimidated. Never had.

But his amused smile stayed put. "Noted."

"And you're not that big," she continued. Childishly, she knew, but she just hadn't been able to stop herself. Because, of course, he was that big. He had to be pushing six-five, and she was fairly certain there wasn't an ounce of body fat on that tall, muscular frame.

The way his mouth seemed to take its time unfurling into an upward curl, the way his dark eyes danced with humor, had unwanted and unfamiliar fireworks going off inside her. Rosalie hated feeling knocked off her axis. She associated it with the aftermath of her father's death, and even if this was a kind of...an almost-pleasant knocked-off-her-axis feeling, she still didn't trust it.

Or him for bringing out unfamiliar feelings.

She patted the gun on her hip. "I'm armed."

KILLER ON THE HOMESTEAD

NICOLE HELM

INTRIGUE

For baseball fans.

INTRIGUE™

Recycling programs for this product may not exist in your area.

ISBN-13: 978-1-335-69013-5

Killer on the Homestead

Harlequin Enterprises ULC
22 Adelaide St. West, 41st Floor
Toronto, Ontario M5H 4E3, Canada
www.Harlequin.com

Printed in Lithuania

MIX
Paper | Supporting responsible forestry
FSC® C021394

Nicole Helm grew up with her nose in a book and the dream of one day becoming a writer. Luckily, after a few failed career choices, she gets to follow that dream—writing down-to-earth contemporary romance and romantic suspense. From farmers to cowboys, Midwest to *the* West, Nicole writes stories about people finding themselves and finding love in the process. She lives in Missouri with her husband and two sons, and dreams of someday owning a barn.

Books by Nicole Helm

Harlequin Intrigue

Bent County Protectors

Vanishing Point
Killer on the Homestead

Hudson Sibling Solutions

Cold Case Kidnapping
Cold Case Identity
Cold Case Investigation
Cold Case Scandal
Cold Case Protection
Cold Case Discovery
Cold Case Murder Mystery

Covert Cowboy Soldiers

The Lost Hart Triplet
Small Town Vanishing
One Night Standoff
Shot in the Dark
Casing the Copycat
Clandestine Baby

Visit the Author Profile page at Harlequin.com.

CAST OF CHARACTERS

Rosalie Young—Private investigator with Fool's Gold Investigations. Lives on a ranch, next to the Kirks, with her sister and cousin.

Duncan Kirk—Former professional baseball player who is back home on the ranch after an injury ended his playing career. Seeks out Rosalie's help at his mother's request.

Norman and Natalie Kirk—Duncan's parents, who run the Kirk Ranch.

Audra Young—Rosalie's older sister. Rancher.

Franny Perkins—Rosalie's cousin. Writer.

Owen Green—Ranch hand at the Kirk Ranch. Friend of Hunter Villanova, who was recently murdered on the Kirk Ranch.

Terry Boothe—Longtime foreman at the Kirk Ranch.

Laurel Delaney-Carson, Thomas Hart and Copeland Beckett—Detectives at the Bent County Sheriff's Department.

Chapter One

Duncan Kirk stood in the front yard of his childhood home while his dad chattered on about the improvements they'd made to the old foreman's cabin.

He would have rented a car and driven himself, or hell, bought one, but he'd only just gotten cleared to move from an immobilizer to a soft sling for his shoulder. The drive would have been too long and too painful on his own.

He could have hired a driver, but no matter how much money he had to spare, his parents would have seen it as an insult.

So his father had picked him up at the airport and driven him…home.

Funny to think of Bent County, Wyoming, as home when he'd barely spent more than a handful of holidays at his family's ranch since he'd left for college.

But it was home, all the same. Because baseball had been home for these odd fifteen years, and now it was gone. Duncan hadn't really thought about or missed the ranch or Wyoming in all this time, but now that he was here…

It was surprisingly comforting.

The house didn't look the same. Nothing really did. Bent County had expanded and grown, and his parents' ranch had come along with the times.

But still, it was nothing like his house back in LA, his *life* in California. The life he was returning to was nothing like the world he'd been living in for almost half his life.

Six months ago, he'd been pitching in front of a sold-out crowd in Dodger Stadium. World Series. Game seven. The moment every little kid who loves baseball dreams of. It was supposed to be his crowning achievement. Oh, he'd thought he had a few years left in him, but he knew he was reaching the peak of what he could do.

Age would take him eventually, but not yet. Or so he'd thought.

He'd gone through his normal warm-up, been amped and buzzed at the noise of the home crowd. He'd visualized a complete-game shutout, obviously. He wasn't too greedy to think of a perfect game. He'd have been happy with anything that resulted in a win, but in the pregame, it was all about seeing the end. Knowing it was within his grasp.

He'd taken the field. Stared down the intimidating lead-off hitter known for his power *and* speed. Then he'd thrown one pitch, felt a terrifying *snap* in his shoulder that had sent a numbness down his entire arm, and watched the ball sail over the catcher's head.

He'd come out of the game. His team had lost.

And his career was over.

Really over. The doctors had made that clear. He might get his shoulder back to functioning in a somewhat normal capacity, with lots of work and years of healing, but not the kind of shape that could throw a ball over eighty miles an hour, and with the kids coming up these days topping triple digits, he didn't have a prayer.

Everything he'd worked for since he could remember was gone. It was always coming for him, that inevitable end. He just wished he'd had some *say* in the when, and the how.

Instead, he was back in Wyoming. Still a young man, all things considered, but feeling old and wrung out.

When his mother opened the front door and stepped onto the porch while drying her hands on a dishrag, a wave of love and nostalgia swept over him strong enough to make him smile and forget the dull pain in his shoulder.

He walked up to the porch as she walked down the stairs. She enveloped him in a tight hug, though she was careful about his left shoulder. "Welcome home, sweetheart."

For a moment, he just stayed there. He didn't know what the hell to do with his life without baseball, but his steady, stable parents and the sight of the ranch that had been in their family for well over a century reminded him that he'd figure it out.

He pulled back, smiled down at his mother. "Good to see you, Mom."

"You would have seen me sooner if you'd let me fly down for your surgery," she said, swatting him with the dish towel. "Come on now, dinner's waiting."

It was four o'clock in the afternoon, but he wouldn't say no to his mother's cooking. He walked inside, Dad trailing behind and bringing in his bags, even though Duncan had told him he'd handle it.

It was going to take some getting used to, being back with his parents who did as they pleased. But at least he wasn't staying in the main house. None of them would survive that. The cabin that had been built for a foreman generations back would suit. A lot smaller and more rustic than he was used to, but that was fine.

He took a seat at the dining-room table Mom had already set. He let her fuss, mostly because she liked it and partly because his shoulder was killing him. It was time for another painkiller, but he needed to eat before he took the pill.

And to not take it around his parents. His mother would fuss no matter what, but he wanted to keep the fussing to a minimum. If she knew he was still in a lot of pain…

Well, he'd be back in his childhood bedroom, and that wasn't going to fly.

They ate together much like they did when he came home for Thanksgiving or Christmas. Dad talked about the ranch. Mom caught him up on the goings-on in Bent County, though he only remembered half the names she mentioned. The Youngs still lived next door, though Tim had died and Joan had moved to Florida. Their daughters ran the ranch now, though mostly the oldest, Audra.

He remembered Audra as a serious girl with serious eyes, a year or two behind him in school. The younger sister, Rosalie, had been the polar opposite. He remembered, with some fondness, when she'd punched one of his high-school teammates for trying to cop a feel on the bus.

She was a private investigator, according to Mom, at some place in Wilde. Duncan wasn't surprised at that. The main things he remembered about Rosalie Young were her red hair and the way she always liked to stick her nose into trouble.

Mom told him about an issue with a cousin of theirs not too long ago, and even bigger trouble a while back, when the mysterious Hudson family disappearance had been solved after years of being a cold case. Which had led to the gruesome discovery of years of dead bodies in a cave in the state park.

Mom claimed she'd told him about all this already, but he didn't remember it. In fairness, he didn't pay attention to much aside from baseball when the season was in full swing. Or in the offseason, when he was already planning on the next season.

Now there was nothing to plan for.

He really thought he'd moved a little closer to acceptance in the past few months of doctor's appointments and discussions of options, then surgery and the inevitable bad news, but something about being home was like finally fully admitting defeat. Even more so than the retirement announcement he'd had to make.

He was *not* going to deal with that horrible sinking feeling at his parents' dinner table. He'd wait until he was alone in the cabin, tucked away for the night.

Dad's phone chimed, and Duncan was surprised to see his father check it without one admonition from his mother. They shared a look and Dad scooted back in his chair.

"I've got to go check on some things. I'll be back."

Duncan watched his father go, then looked at his mother, who was staring very hard at her plate.

"What's wrong?" Because he could think of no other reason his mother would accept anyone reading a text at her dinner table *and* then leaving, unless it was an emergency.

He watched his mother consider her answer. Then look over her shoulder as if to make sure Dad was gone. "It's nothing."

Which was clearly a bald-faced lie. "Mom."

She sighed. "He won't want me to tell you." She looked over her shoulder again. "He's already mad at me for being pushy."

"Pushy? You?"

She scorched him with a mean look in response to his sarcasm. "We've had some cows disappear is all."

"Disappearing? How do cows disappear?"

Mom waved away the question. "Dad'll figure it out."

She smiled, but there was some worry in the new lines on her face. "Except…" She sighed. "You have to pretend I didn't tell you."

"Scout's honor."

"You weren't a Scout, Duncan," she said, but she almost smiled at the old joke. "It's just strange. In all our years of ranching, we've never seen such a thing. Because cows just don't go *missing*. Not one by one like this."

"Is someone taking them?"

"That's one theory."

"If someone's stealing them, why hasn't he called the police?"

"We don't know for certain anyone's stealing them. It may be a bad spot in the fence. Or maybe some silly prank." She sighed. "Dad talked to Sheriff Hudson, but that's Sunrise, and we're unincorporated. Bent County is who Dad would need to file a report with, and he's stubborn. Doesn't like their new 'modern' sensibility. I guess they hired a detective from Denver, over that good-for-nothing cousin of his's kid." Mom shook her head disgustedly. She had no fondness for some of Dad's extended family.

But Duncan wasn't interested in old family feuds. "So what's he doing about it then?"

"Worry himself to death," Mom said with a scowl. She sighed, leaned close and lowered her voice, even though Dad was long gone. "He's afraid he's getting old and forgetful. He even went to the doctor of his own accord."

Duncan was surprised at how hard that hit him. Once Dad had broken his arm and refused to go to the doctor for *days*. Until Mom had threatened to knock him out and drag him to the hospital herself.

"Nothing came back, except a bit of high cholesterol, go figure. But he's still embarrassed that something's going on under his nose. Worried. Blaming himself. I've tried to get him to call Bent County. I've talked to the ranch hands, tried to get them to convince him to call, but... Well, you know your father."

"Stubborn is an understatement."

She smiled fondly. "He certainly didn't pass that trait on."

Duncan grunted.

"I did have one idea, but he'd be so angry with me if I butted my nose in even more than I already have."

"I've never known you to care about getting Dad's temper up," Duncan said. He meant it as a joke, but Mom didn't smile, laugh, or have any of her usual responses.

He suddenly *felt* the years he'd been away. And the fact that no matter that he'd always come home for holidays, or flown his parents out for a visit and a game, it was a lot different than living under the same roof. Or even in the same state.

Mom looked down at her hand. Her left hand, where the simple wedding band she'd worn for almost forty years had always been. "It's weighing on him, and it's weighing on us," she said very quietly.

Quiet enough that Duncan's whole stomach knotted and knotted hard. The idea that his parents might have marriage problems was just...

God-awful.

She inhaled deeply, then looked up at him with her usual smile. Though he thought he saw a shininess in her dark eyes, which made the knot of dread in his gut tighten. His mother didn't *cry.* At least not in front of people.

"But you know, his only child, freshly moved home. Well...he might not be so angry at him."

Duncan blinked. He didn't particularly like the idea of

crossing his father either. "You want me to…do what exactly?"

"Talk to Rosalie."

He wrinkled his nose. "The neighbor girl?"

"She's not a *girl* any longer. She's a private investigator with a company in Wilde, like I just told you. Maybe she could look into this without Dad knowing. Sheriff Hudson said there hadn't been any other missing cattle in the area, but maybe Rosalie could just…look into it. *I* can't ask her to do it—it would get back to Dad—but *you* could."

Normally he'd balk at the idea of getting involved. Usually, he'd talk to his dad himself. But everything about this conversation had him unsettled and he just wanted to make everything easy and right.

"Sure, Mom. I will. Don't even worry about it. I'll handle everything."

He didn't have baseball anymore, so maybe this was his new thing to focus on.

DUNCAN WOKE UP LATE, the sunlight streaming in through his window. No doubt Dad would have a few comments about *that*, but he'd probably spent more of last night awake and in pain than sleeping.

Duncan pushed himself up in bed and cursed the dull ache in his shoulder. Cursed a lot of things on his way to the tiny kitchen of the cabin—his new *home*. He had the presence of mind to set up the coffeepot last night, so all he had to do this morning was press a button and wait for it to brew. Mom had stocked the pantry and fridge, including some breakfast sandwiches he only needed to pop in the microwave.

Bacon, egg, and cheese with a homemade biscuit. Not exactly the kind of food that he usually allowed himself.

He'd always been so determined to stay in the best physical shape he could—exercise, diet, limited alcohol.

Fat lot of good that had done, he thought grumpily.

But once he'd eaten, sucked down two mugs of coffee and taken his pain pill, he felt better and more like taking on the day. He could unpack, but that sounded horrible. He doubted he'd be much help around the ranch with his shoulder in a sling. The thought of riding a horse like this had him wincing.

So he figured the best option for his day was to drive out to Wilde and see about Rosalie Young and private investigators.

He texted his mother that he was taking her car—she'd given him an extra set of keys. Maybe he'd take a detour to Fairmont and see if the car dealer there had anything that'd work for him long-term. None of the cars he'd kept in LA would survive ranch life, so he'd sold them off.

He drove off the ranch. It was a cloudy spring day, and rain started to spit from the sky about halfway to Wilde. He preferred that to sunny blue skies, which reminded him of summers at the ballpark.

Wilde was still little more than a postage stamp of a town. Duncan didn't know how they managed to have an actual private investigator's business here. He supposed the historical tours that started here and wound around Bent County might help with that, but it wasn't like they had much else to offer.

He pulled into a parking spot along the street. The office was in some kind of historical building, and had no doubt been something else in the past. Maybe a bank? He jogged inside to avoid as much of the rain as possible.

Inside, it smelled like fresh paint, and there were a lot of pretty feminine touches. There was a woman behind the big counter, but he wouldn't say *feminine* as a descriptor quite fit her.

She looked…tough. Wild. Pretty, no doubt, but not like she'd been the woman to arrange the flowers on the counter or put potpourri out on tables. Then again, looks could be deceiving.

The woman glanced up from whatever she was typing into her computer, but her gaze was distracted. "Be with you in a second." She immediately looked back down, then stilled, sneaking a glance at him. He watched as the recognition crossed her face. Then, with some amusement, watched as she decided how to handle it.

He was used to it, to an extent. He didn't like the new layer of *embarrassment* that went with people recognizing him, but still. He'd been a young phenom with plenty of attention, then a young man with a record-breaking contract, and he'd lived the high life in LA when he'd wanted to. So he got noticed.

But it was still weird back here, where he felt more like a kid with big dreams than the adult who'd achieved them. Then lost them.

When she addressed him, her smile was bland, and any reaction she'd had to recognizing him was hidden behind an easy smile. "What can I do you for?"

"I don't suppose Rosalie Young is here?"

"You know Rosalie?" the woman replied, studying him carefully.

"Sort of. We're neighbors. Or were, growing up."

"Huh." She shrugged. "Rosalie's out, but I can leave her a message for you."

Duncan considered. Would leaving a message get back to Dad? Bent County itself wasn't a small town, it was a large, sprawling county made up of ranches, mountains, and a handful of small and almost medium-size towns, but he knew the way information snaked through those places. One to the other.

"Do you know when she'll be back?"

The woman looked up at the wall behind him, so he did too. There was a big old clock up on it. "Sometime this afternoon."

"Maybe you could give me her phone number."

The woman's expression hardened a little. "I can give you her extension. You're welcome to leave a message on her work line."

Duncan considered that. It would be private if it was her own extension. But before he could decide what to do, a bell on the door tinkled. He turned and watched as a redhead whirled into the lobby.

"If that lousy SOB had talked instead of giving me the runaround, I wouldn't be caught in a damn downpour," she muttered as she wiped her boots on a mat by the door.

Sure, she wasn't the only person in the world with red hair and blue eyes that leaned toward violet, but he knew it was her.

And that on an adult woman all those little details landed…differently, in a kind of *jolt*. Because she didn't have skinned knees and falling-out braids any longer. She was dressed in tight jeans, heavy boots, and a black T-shirt. He didn't know much about guns that weren't meant for hunting, and even then, he'd never been into it. But he knew she had one strapped to a holster on her hip. She was short, with a medium build, but something about the way she carried herself gave the aura of someone taller, someone who could kick ass.

But her face somehow looked delicate on that tough package. Maybe it was the raindrops in her hair and on her face that seemed to tease out the little smattering of freckles across her nose.

Something about the whole of her was surprisingly *attractive*. Not that he had the time or presence of mind to be noticing just how attractive. Even if it *had* been a while in that department, and he—

No. He was here to help out his parents. Not flirt with the neighbor girl.

Who, as his mother had pointed out, was not a *girl* anymore.

He saw the recognition on her face right away, and in the slight pause in her stride. But her expression didn't give away much more than that. Just that she recognized him.

He didn't know what possessed him then. He hadn't seen her in something like fifteen years, and it wasn't like they'd been friends or even enemies. They'd been neighbors. Their parents had been friends. And they'd had to take the same interminable bus ride into school for the years they'd been going at the same time, which was quite a few since the bus ran ranch kids in kindergarten all the way up to seniors in high school.

But an old memory struck him, of someone calling her Rosie, and her coming unglued. And no doubt it was a *bad* instinct, but he leaned into it anyway.

"Heya, Rosie. Long time, no see."

Chapter Two

Rosalie Young stared at the outrageously handsome man standing in the lobby of Fool's Gold Investigations and didn't let any of the feelings rambling around inside of her show on her face.

His dark hair looked a little windswept, and longer than he kept it during the season. He'd grown a beard, but she wondered if that was more because of the sling his arm was in rather than any choice in the matter. His dark eyes were focused, intelligent, and a little amused. His mouth… Well, his mouth was an interesting mix of all sorts of things that might have normally had her offering a flirtatious smile.

But this was Duncan Kirk. Hometown boy turned baseball superstar.

Even though she'd watched his career with interest—who wouldn't cheer on the hometown kid?—she still had the mental picture of him as the grumpy little cuss who'd lived on the ranch next door.

Maybe grumpy wasn't fair, she could admit, with years of growing up under her belt. She didn't know much about professional sports, but she knew for anyone to get out of a ranch in the middle of nowhere Wyoming and become a professional athlete took a lot more than luck.

Maybe he hadn't been so much *grumpy* as focused, she had amended a few years back.

Still, she preferred thinking about a grumpy teen as opposed to when she'd last seen him. On a TV screen. Along with a lot of people in Bent County, shoved into Rightful Claim, ordering beers and ready to cheer on the hometown kid.

Only to watch him all but collapse in pain after one pitch.

It was hard to be ticked that he'd called her *Rosie* when she remembered that, and all the subsequent stories about a man's amazing career being cut short. Especially when he was wearing a sling, which was the same color as the T-shirt he was wearing, so it *almost* blended in.

But not quite.

"Duncan," she offered. She looked at her boss, Quinn, who ran Fool's Gold. Quinn shrugged like she didn't know why he was here either. "Having some trouble you need investigated?"

"Actually…" Duncan looked back at Quinn. "Maybe. You got somewhere to talk in private?"

"Sure." She moved past him, and ignored the little jolt to her system when, underneath the flowery smell of potpourri that Quinn's sister put out in the lobby, she caught a hint of piney aftershave and afternoon rain.

Whatever. Rich guys *should* smell good. She didn't tell him to follow her, or gesture him to, but he did all the same. She led him into her office. Only she and Quinn were full-time employees right now, so they both had their own offices. There were two other rooms with doors off the lobby that part-time investigators could use to talk to clients, interrogate witnesses, or whatever else was needed.

Maybe she should have taken him into one of those

rooms, she thought as he moved into her space and started studying her array of desk pictures, but it was too late now. He was already staring at the newest addition. A picture from her second cousin's wedding last month. Vi looked pretty as a picture in her simple white dress, holding her one-year-old. Thomas Hart, her husband, was handsome in his suit, the jacket hiding his own sling after he'd been shot trying to save Vi just a few weeks before the wedding.

Audra, Franny, and Rosalie fanned out next to them in their spring dresses, smiling at the camera, the Young Ranch and mountains spread out behind them.

It had been a good day. A healing day. Rosalie wanted to remember it always. But there was something about Duncan Kirk looking at that moment captured in the picture, knowing some of the players, but not all, that felt…weird.

She closed the door, took one quick second to settle herself, then turned to look at him. He'd stopped staring at her pictures and was studying her.

"We tend to lean toward helping women," she began. Which wasn't the kindest way to ask him what he was after.

"Well, in a way you would be, since it's my mother who sent me."

She raised an eyebrow as she moved behind her desk. "Your mother is not the kind of woman who sends someone else to do her dirty work."

"No, she isn't."

He didn't offer anything else. She sat and motioned for him to do the same on the other side of her desk.

He looked at the chair, the desk, the picture, then sighed and took a seat. She couldn't quite read him. So she waited for him to explain.

She tried very hard not to fidget when it took a lot longer than she considered *polite*. "I don't have *all* day, Duncan."

"Right. There's been some trouble at my parents' ranch. Some missing cows. I don't suppose you've heard anything about it?"

"I can't say that I keep up with the ranch gossip. That's Audra's department." Which still left Rosalie feeling guilty. She loved the ranch, but as an abstract. As a home. Not as a business to see to.

Which meant all the nuts and bolts of running that ranch fell on her older sister's tough and capable, but way over-worked, shoulders.

"I guess, one by one, cows have been disappearing from the ranch. Dad was worried he was just getting…forget-ful. He talked to Sheriff Hudson in Sunrise, but he hadn't heard of any found cows. I guess he doesn't like some de-tective from Denver being at Bent County, so he doesn't want to call there."

"Yeah, Beckett ruffles some feathers, but he's not all bad," Rosalie responded. She worked with a lot of the depu-ties and detectives in Bent County. Or harassed them into giving her information. Copeland Beckett wasn't her favor-ite, but watching him work on her cousin's case last month had softened her a bit in that department. That and the fact that Vi's husband worked with and trusted him.

Still, it read fishy to her that Mr. Kirk didn't want to call the actual cops, who might be able to help him.

"My mom's worried," Duncan continued. "About him. About the missing cows. She just wants someone to look into it. See if it *could* be someone purposefully taking those cows."

"Problem with that theory is a few months back, Audra found some of your dad's cattle on our land. Looked like a fence had just been left open. Nothing nefarious. The cows were returned."

"Maybe this is different."

"Maybe." But in her experience, cattle rustling wasn't much of a money maker around these parts. One cow at a time didn't exactly scream criminal plot. "Any ranch hands suspect?"

"Mom didn't think so, but I don't really know the players. Except my father."

"And it's not possible that it's an honest mistake?"

Duncan's mouth firmed. The slight flicker of anger and the ticking muscle in his jaw were far more attractive than they had a right to be.

Yeah, she had issues. She knew it.

"No," he said firmly.

"Look, this isn't the type of case I usually take on. I'll do it for your mom. But I like my clients to know they might not like the answers they want me to find. That sometimes, the most obvious answer we don't want *is* the answer."

"My dad isn't rustling his own cows, and he's not careless."

Rosalie shrugged. "It'll be my job to determine that myself. You need to be prepared for it to be either of those things."

"My father's the most honest man I know."

It left a pang in her heart. She would have said the same about her dad. But hero worship was a hell of a thing. It blinded a person to…everything. She pushed aside all that buried past.

"Look, I'm not saying I won't take the case."

He scowled. "For a price."

She didn't mind the hint of bitterness in his tone. She was too sure of herself and what she did to be hurt by someone else's opinion of it. "It's my job, Ace. And last I checked, you could afford it."

"Yeah, when was the last time you checked?"

There were a lot of ways she could take that question. A lot of ways she could answer it. But in typical Rosalie fashion, she took the one that hurt. Besides, he *had* called her *Rosie*, and no doubt remembered that she hated that nickname. "Y'all had a heck of a postseason run."

His expression became guarded. She'd somehow known it would. "Something like that."

"You pitched a hell of a game one. Four wasn't bad either."

Now he scowled. "I know it."

She didn't mind putting that scowl there any more than she minded the pride, and maybe ego, that went into the *I know it*. First, because she was a little perverse and found a pissed-off man hotter than she should. Second, because she needed him to understand she wasn't doing a favor, and this might not go the way he wanted. *She* certainly wouldn't be putty in his hands like he was no doubt used to.

"I'll dig around a little, see if there's anything fishy going on. You only have to pay me for my time. I won't hose you, even if you can afford it."

He huffed out a bit of a laugh. "I guess we'll see."

Rosalie currently had two cases going. One was simple enough. A woman had hired her to prove her husband's philandering ways. The other one was a little bit more complicated, as it involved a very *careful* stalker who knew his victim had gone to the cops. It was a pretty full plate, and she shouldn't take on Duncan's case, but...

Mrs. Kirk had been more than kind to Rosalie and her family. Especially after Dad died. Natalie Kirk had even tried to convince Mom to stay. Rosalie knew the Kirks helped Audra a lot on the ranch side of things and never made it seem like a big deal or an inconvenience.

Maybe the current facts pointed to Mr. Kirk, in Rosalie's estimation, but she supposed if she found that out, the Kirks could deal with it. They'd have to.

She knew all about uncomfortable truths.

On her way home, she decided to stop by Bent and kill a few birds with one stone. She parked her truck in the Bent County Sheriff's Department lot, locked her gun away, then went inside.

Thomas Hart was manning the information desk. He looked up as she walked in. Normally a detective, he'd been shot in the line of duty last month, so he was chained to his desk for a while yet.

"Hey, Hart."

"Hey, Rosalie."

"How's the arm?" she asked, leaning against the counter of the desk.

He scowled. "Horrible."

"How's the wife?"

Said scowl turned into a grin. "Amazing. I am a well-fed man."

She glared at him. Because his wife, *her* second cousin, had once lived on the Young Ranch with *her* and used her considerable cooking skills to feed Rosalie. "Bragger."

"I aim to be when it comes to Vi and Mags."

And since the simple sweet *love* imbued in each of those words made her itchy, she got to the point. "You got a copy of that police report on the property damage I requested?"

He swiveled in his chair, pulled out a file folder, and handed it to her. "No leads. Not sure how that's going to help your case."

She shrugged, flipped through the file to make sure everything she requested was there. Hart was okay to work with, but some of the deputies sneered at what she did. She figured they were jealous she could bend the laws they had to enforce to get her perps. "We'll see." She closed the file, looked at Hart.

"You heard of any cattle rustling going on?"

His expression immediately changed to one of concern. "Something happen at the ranch?"

She shook her head. "Not at our place. This is Fool's Gold business."

He leaned back in his chair, blew out a breath. "Haven't heard anything that I can think of off the top of my head, but I'll ask around. Let you know."

"Thanks. How many more weeks you got back here?"

He grunted. "Got a doctor's appointment next week. Hoping to wheedle some clearance out of him."

"Good luck, then. See you Sunday."

"Vi's bringing rolls and pasta salad."

"Thank God," Rosalie said, and meant it. "Audra can bake, but she can't cook for a damn."

"You should tell her that."

"Ha. Ha." Rosalie left the sheriff's department and drove back to the Young Ranch, out closer to the small town of Sunrise. She pulled off the highway onto a side road, then onto the gravel road that would lead her home.

There was a sign under the arch that read *Young Ranch, Established 1908.* She loved this place. In her bones. She didn't care a whit about raising cattle, the price of beef or hay. She wanted nothing to do with the accounting books or inventory, but she *loved* the place. The feeling of ancestry and history and just…home.

Even if her parents had turned out to be the opposite of

everything she'd thought, it didn't tarnish the love she felt for this *place*. For roots.

And it had been nice, really, just her and Audra and their cousin, Franny. Three twentysomething women living together, kicking Wyoming ass together. They'd helped Vi out of her terrible situation, gotten to help raise Magnolia before Vi had moved in with Thomas. Life was good.

Good.

She heard voices the minute she walked into the main house. The welcome smell of meat sizzling in the kitchen— which meant Franny had cooked, thank goodness. She dropped her bag, took two steps, then wrinkled her nose and turned back to hang it up on the hook, as Audra preferred.

Sometimes she liked bothering her older sister. Sometimes she lived for it. And sometimes Audra's long-suffering self-sacrifice made Rosalie feel like a guilty slob.

Once her bag had been hung up acceptably, she moved into the kitchen. Audra and Franny were already sitting at the table, plates full.

They greeted each other and Rosalie went straight for the food and began to pile her plate high. There was nothing better than a home-cooked meal after a day of work. Especially when Franny was making it.

"I heard someone talking about Duncan Kirk being in town," Franny said in between bites as Rosalie slid into her seat at the table.

Audra nodded. "Natalie told me he's planning to stay indefinitely. They even fixed up one of the cabins on their property for him."

"That's next *door*. Do you think we'll see him?" Franny had grown up in Seattle with Audra and Rosalie's aunt and uncle, but they'd always made the trek out to Wyoming for holidays. Audra and Franny especially had kept in touch as teenagers, and when Franny's writing career had taken off, she'd moved out to Wyoming to live with them for a bit. For *inspiration*, she said.

Rosalie thought about Duncan Kirk in her office this afternoon. He would be one hell of an inspiration. "*I* saw him," Rosalie volunteered. "Talked to him even."

Both Audra and Franny whipped their gazes to her. "You did?"

Rosalie realized that even telling them he'd come to Fool's Gold was a little too close to ruining the client privacy she worked very hard to keep. "Yep. Ran right into him on the street."

"You talked to him?" Audra asked.

"Is he as hot in person as he is on the TV?" Franny demanded.

Rosalie grinned at Franny. "Hotter."

"Impossible."

Rosalie shook her head, kind of enjoying herself. "Swear it. His hair's a little shaggy. He's got a beard going on."

"Not a beard." Franny groaned and put a hand to her heart, making Audra and Rosalie laugh.

Conversation turned to *other* hot guys with beards— locals and celebrities. Franny told them some about her newest book idea—with details she'd gotten from pumping Hart for detective stories. Once they were done eating, Rosalie took her chore of cleaning up the dishes while Audra packed up the leftovers.

"You were nice, weren't you?" Audra asked.

Rosalie frowned at her sister, irritated she knew just what Audra was talking about. And tried not to feel guilty for kind of making it sound like Mr. Kirk might be his own problem. "What's that supposed to mean?"

"It means I know you. The Kirks have been so good to us. I just want to make sure you remember that. Even if Duncan hasn't been around, he's a Kirk."

"I'm not a total jerk, Audra."

"That's not what I'm saying," Audra replied. But she didn't say *of course you're not a jerk, Rosalie.*

Which probably shouldn't grate as much as it did. And it only grated because she *was* kind of a jerk. She liked to think she'd earned it, and it kept people from taking advantage of her, like they did with Audra when Rosalie wasn't around to run interference.

But Audra, with her impeccable eldest-sister abilities, knew just how to twist an unintended knife.

Rosalie spent half the night looking into the Kirks' cattle operation.

Chapter Three

Duncan spent the next few days getting settled into his new life. He bought a truck. Bought some new clothes more suited for life on the ranch. He unpacked one box, but that was depressing as hell, so he ignored the rest.

He ate dinner with his parents every night. He hadn't been planning on that, but Mom seemed to expect it, and he couldn't deny he was worried about his parents. It didn't sound like any more cattle had disappeared, and he hadn't heard from Rosalie at all.

But he'd thought about her. And not in an is-she-researching-missing-cattle kind of way. More like, is she single and is this too complicated?

He had a demanding life, or he'd *had* a demanding life, so he was very well versed in what he liked to call *risk management* when it came to women.

Rosalie was intertwined in his parents' life. That one fact was reason enough to keep his thoughts to himself. But thoughts—and fantasies—never hurt anyone, did they?

When Dad said he was going back out to check the fences with a couple of his hands before sundown, Duncan offered to help Mom with the dishes even though it was usually Dad's job.

If he cast back among all his memories of his parents,

it was that simple after-dinner routine that made him feel the most centered, the most…*home.* Dad sitting on a stool at the sink, rinsing off dishes and putting them in the dishwasher while Mom put the leftovers away and cleaned up the cooking debris.

"I don't suppose you've heard anything from Rosalie about the cattle?" she asked as he dutifully put plates in the dishwasher.

"She said she'd look into it."

"It's been days."

"Maybe it takes days to look into stuff." Though he supposed he could call her tomorrow. Test the waters.

The *investigation* waters. Nothing else. He tossed the detergent pod into the dishwasher and closed the door. When he turned to his mother, she was holding out a paper grocery bag.

"Why don't you go on over to the Young house. Take this over. That Audra runs herself ragged. It's always my pleasure when I can send some extras her way."

Mom had already packed up a bag of their dinner leftovers—leftovers they only had because Mom no doubt had made enough to ensure there was food left to take to the Youngs. She shoved it at him. He grabbed it with one arm, his other arm throbbing. He considered using it as an excuse, but before he could, Mom looked at his sling. Considered.

"Well, I suppose I can do it. I'm supposed to lead the church meeting tonight, but…"

"I'll do it," he grumbled, not letting her take the bag back.

"Only if you're sure you're up to it. I'm sure driving with the sling isn't comfortable and—"

"It's fine."

"That's my boy." She patted his cheek. "I'm going to go wash up. You run that out to them before they eat."

He knew he'd been maneuvered when she bounced off like she'd never had a care in the world about his arm. He was going to have to relearn how to fend off his mother's machinations.

But for this evening, he took his punishment and the food and drove the access road from the Kirk house to the Young house, cursing his shoulder every time he hit a bump, or when he had to get out and open and close the gate.

It hurt like hell, but at the same time it felt better than those first few weeks when he'd just been moping around his place in LA. Something about fresh air, sunlight, and mountains, maybe.

Or maybe it was just being home.

He drove onto the gravel lane that wound up to the Young place. Unlike his childhood home, their house looked exactly as he remembered it. A little on the small side, with a big rambling porch. Mountains rose up in the distance, like guarding sentries looming over everything.

Two redheads sat on the porch swing, heads bent together. One—Audra, he was guessing—had her legs crossed and was sitting upright. The other—Rosalie, definitely—was lounging, using her bare foot, which was on the porch railing, to move the swing back and forth.

They watched as his truck approached, then him. Rosalie was drinking a beer out of a bottle, and Audra had a glass of something. They didn't look a heck of a lot alike, except for their coloring. Both were redheads, though Audra's ran closer to brown. Both had those too-blue eyes, though Audra's were smaller and closer set than Rosalie's. Audra was tall and willowy, he noted as she got to her feet.

Then swatted her sister when she didn't do the same.

"It's good to see you again, Duncan," she offered politely, as she walked over to the top of the stairs. Rosalie stayed on the swing and said nothing.

"You too, Audra." He held up the bag. "Hope you guys didn't eat yet. Mom sent me over with leftovers."

"Thank *God*," Rosalie said under her breath, earning her a scolding look from Audra.

"*You* could learn to cook," Audra said to her sister as she took the bag from Duncan.

"Can't. No patience," Rosalie replied, and it was clearly an old argument without much heat. But she flashed a grin at Duncan as she said it that made a disconcerting bolt of lust go through him.

Disconcerting because her sister was right there, and because she was connected to his family in a weird kind of way. And with the cow-investigation thing, it certainly wasn't smart to be distracted by a quick smile and pretty eyes.

But even with those alarm bells ringing, it was kind of a relief, because it had been a long time since anything—including a woman—had distracted him from his laser-beam focus.

"Thank your mom for me, Duncan," Audra said. "We really do appreciate everything she does for us."

"She likes it, or she wouldn't do it, but I'll tell her."

"I'll just go put this away. And I'll warn you to run out of here rather than spend even a second in small talk with my feral hog of a sister."

"*Hog?*" Rosalie huffed. "Rude."

Audra just smirked and went inside. He watched her go, noting more differences in the sisters. Audra didn't have that…*swagger* Rosalie wore like a second skin.

Rosalie cleared her throat, and he turned his attention to her, but she didn't say anything. So he did.

"Y'all should have a guard dog."

"Franny's allergic."

"Who's Franny?"

"Oh, our other roommate. Our cousin on our mom's side. Besides, who needs a guard dog when we're all carrying and excellent shots?" She grinned at him, all sharp angles and implied threat. "Audra wins sharpshooting trophies on the regular."

Maybe there was something wrong with him that he was very interested in every last one of her implied threats.

She finally got up off the swing and walked over to the steps. "Sorry I haven't been in touch. Had another case get hot. I did do some initial looking into everything though. I haven't forgotten about you. Just haven't found much to go on. Except I did run background checks on some of your dad's ranch hands. He's got a newer one. Owen Green. He had a few brushes with the law when he was a minor."

"I'm not saying it's not worth looking into, but most of the younger guys who work for my dad are his brothers' or cousins' ne'er-do-well kids. Mom calls it Norman's Camp for Wayward Boys."

Rosalie chuckled. "Yeah. I've heard the complaints. I didn't realize this one was one of his though."

"Pretty sure Green is a North Dakota cousin. But by all means, look into him. I don't trust them any more than my mom does."

"Will do, boss."

"So how much do I owe you? Or do you just bill me when you're done? And make sure it's me. I don't want Mom seeing the cost."

She lifted a shoulder. "Free of charge."

"I thought I could afford it."

"Audra lectured me about how great your parents have been to us since…" She trailed off, never finishing that sentence.

But he knew. Maybe he hadn't remembered all the details, but Mom had been filling him in. When Tim Young had died, it came out that he'd been having an affair for quite a few years. He had a whole second family out in Cheyenne no one had known about. Then his actual wife had left the girls with the ranch, not wanting to be around anything that reminded her of Tim.

Including her daughters.

Apparently the Young girls—*women*, he had to keep reminding himself—had tried to make some overtures with their half siblings in the time since, but that hadn't worked out.

Audra popped her head out of the door. "Duncan, have you eaten? You're more than welcome to come in and join us."

"No, I ate. Thanks. Enjoy the food. I'll see y'all around." He gave a bit of a wave, and one last glance at Rosalie, then turned back to his truck. He was about halfway there when Rosalie spoke.

"Hey, one more thing." She hopped down the stairs and took a few strides toward him. Then, when she was out of earshot of the front door, she spoke quietly. She pointed a finger at him. "You check out my sister again and I'll castrate you."

He supposed he should take that as the warning it was meant to be. He *supposed* he should let the comment slide and get out of there. But she was standing there, chin lifted, arms folded over her chest. The falling sunlight made her hair look especially…fiery.

He supposed a lot of men were intimidated by her. Maybe he should be. But he couldn't seem to find it in himself. "What if it was you that I was checking out?"

He watched her wrestle with something, hoped at least a *little* of that mischievous sparkle in her eyes was humor, not castration plans.

"Audra's got too soft a heart. Me? Mine's titanium. I can handle myself against the likes of you."

"That feels like a dare, Red."

This time, she couldn't quite stop herself from smiling, though he watched her try. "I'll be in touch, *Ace*," she said, then turned on a heel and strode back inside.

And, yeah, he checked her out the whole way.

HE'D BEEN FLIRTING with her. Not uncommon. While Rosalie intimidated some guys, some took her attitude as a challenge. Duncan seemed to be the latter.

But damn, he was so unfairly good-looking. She didn't mind a good flirt. She didn't mind other things. She wasn't looking for anything serious, ever, but she liked the male species on a very superficial level.

Maybe Audra had dreams of roses and white dresses. Maybe Audra *and* Franny looked at Vi and Thomas and Magnolia a little wistfully.

Rosalie most decidedly did not.

Maybe it was a cliché, maybe it meant she needed therapy, but learning her dad had a whole secret family after he'd died had killed absolutely any trust she held in the male species.

Or at least any trust in her judgment of it. Because Hart was okay, and so clearly in love with Vi. Maybe it wasn't that she didn't believe in love, but more that she didn't trust her own take on it.

Either way. She wasn't looking for anything, and she doubted Mr. Superstar was either. But even a flirtation was complicated with the ways their families overlapped, and the fact she was helping him look into some missing cows.

She didn't mind some complications. A person couldn't in a small community like Bent County. Not if she wanted to get laid on occasion. And she *did*.

But Duncan? Nah, too complicated.

Really, *really* hot though.

She shoved away thoughts of Duncan, or tried to, and ate a delicious meal prepared by his mother with Audra and Franny. Most days, it felt like enough, but some days…usually after a night like last night when they'd had Vi, Hart, and Mags over, it felt a little lonely.

She refused to wallow in that though. She enjoyed her dinner, watched a terrible movie with Franny, then went to bed.

In the morning, she figured her first order of business once she got to work would be to look a little deeper into Owen Green, the ne'er-do-well cousin from North Dakota.

She headed downstairs, lured by the smell of coffee and the sound of voices. Audra was pouring her coffee into a thermos, while Franny rested her head against the table.

"What happened to you?"

She lifted her head. "I was up practically all night."

"Writing?"

"In a matter of speaking," she said around a yawn.

Which meant she'd likely spent her entire night either following some research rabbit trail, or watching Taylor Swift conspiracy-theory videos. Or both.

Rosalie grabbed her own thermos from the cupboard. She filled it, but before she could grab a power bar for breakfast, Audra was shoving a bag at her.

"On your way out, can you return all this Tupperware to Natalie?"

Rosalie looked down at it. She really didn't want to, but that was childish. "I guess."

"I was texting Chloe last night, and I mentioned how Duncan was back. She told me to invite him to the engagement party. So, if you see him, can you do that?"

"Invite him to our friend's party?" Rosalie returned. Chloe was a friend of Audra's going way back. Rosalie worked with Jack's sister at Fool's Gold. And a million other connections that happened in a small town.

"Duncan's new to town, kind of, and it'll give him an opportunity to meet, or remeet, people his age."

"He was a famous professional athlete for *years*, Audra. I'm sure he can meet people on his own."

"Here? This is a different world than LA. He might feel out of place. A casual engagement party is the perfect place to reacquaint himself with old friends or meet new ones. I'm sure Duncan knows Jack."

They were around the same age, so probably. But Rosalie didn't know why it fell on *her* to do the inviting. She almost said it, but she saw the way Audra was moving around the kitchen. Too fast because she had too much to do.

"Everything okay, ranch-wise?"

Audra waved her off. "Sure thing. But it'd help me a lot if you took care of that."

"Yeah. Sure." She glanced at Franny, who was still lying on the table, possibly sleeping. "Why don't I bring home a pizza tonight instead of having anyone cook?"

"Sounds good to me but let us know if you're going to be late."

Rosalie nodded, took a few steps toward the kitchen's exit. Then turned to face her sister.

"You're not like…trying to flirt with him, are you?"

Audra blinked, cocked her head. Her expression was blank enough Rosalie couldn't tell what she felt about that question.

"Why?" she asked, sounding casual even if her gaze was considering. "Would that bother you?"

"Why would it bother me?"

Audra shrugged. "I don't know. But you didn't ask it like 'are you trying to flirt with him?' You voiced it as a negative. 'You're not, are you?'"

"No, I didn't."

Audra looked at Franny, whose eyes were open again. "Didn't she?"

"She did," Franny agreed.

"Traitor," Rosalie muttered, then whirled out of the kitchen. It didn't bother her in the least. Not that she was going to let some puffed-up baseball player touch her sister, but if Audra wanted to flirt, she had every right.

Every right, Rosalie repeated to herself as she got in her car and drove over to the Kirk Ranch house. Not at *all* in a foul mood, because she didn't care about Duncan Kirk or parties or *anything*.

When she pulled up in front of the house, a lot more recently modernized than the Young house, where they scraped by year after year thanks to her selfish parents, she was *not at all happy* to see Duncan standing on the porch.

That leap in her chest was definitely irritation. She got out of the car, grabbed the bag of Tupperware, and marched it right up the stairs.

"Your mom here?"

"No, she went to town for some errands already apparently," he said, holding up a Post-it. "Which is suspicious because she told me I could come by this morning and grab some more coffee. I'm out. I didn't even bring my keys with me." He jiggled the knob in frustration.

"Audra insisted I bring this stuff back this morning," Rosalie said, holding the bag out to him. With a frown, he took it.

"Where am I supposed to put it?"

Rosalie shrugged. "How am I supposed to know? I've got to get to work." But since he was here, she could tell him about the party and then not have to see him until she had something to do with the case to talk to him about. *Professionally.* And if she handled this, she could maybe handle making sure her sister's heart didn't get stomped on by this—this...

Whatever he was. "And...she also wanted me to invite you to this party."

"Party?"

"A friend's thing in a few weeks. It's for an engagement, but really informal. Outdoor backyard barbeque type thing. A bunch of us are going, and Audra thought... You know, since you haven't really lived here for a while, you might want to meet or get reacquainted with someone your age. You probably know the host anyway. Jack Hudson?"

"I played T-ball with Jack."

"See? So you should come."

"Because Audra wants me to?"

Rosalie tried not to growl. "She's just being *nice.* Don't let it go to your head."

His mouth quirked up on one side, a kind of boyish, mischievous smile that had butterflies kicking up a racket in her stomach.

"I like nice."

Butterflies officially grounded. She stepped forward. "You touch nice, I'll—"

"Yeah, I remember the threat. You know, I think much better about invitations when I've had my coffee. Want to go up to Coffee Klatch with me? I've been told a lie that their coffee doesn't taste like gas-station dregs anymore."

Rosalie blinked. She couldn't remember the last time she'd been caught so off guard. Before she could decide what to do with *that* invitation though, she heard a scream.

Both she and Duncan moved toward it simultaneously as a young man came scrambling toward them from the barn, waving both arms.

"Call nine-one-one. Call nine-one-one, now!"

Chapter Four

Once they moved, the excitable ranch hand, whose name Duncan couldn't think of though he was sure he was a relation of some sort, started running away from them, like a dog alerting people to danger. So he and Rosalie followed. Rosalie had her cell out, no doubt already dialing 911.

Running jolted pain through his arm with every step, but the frantic terror in the ranch hand's voice meant he couldn't stop.

Until he saw a body in the pasture. Then he came to a skidding halt, even as Rosalie shoved the phone at him and rushed forward. She went right up to that bloody body and kneeled down next to it. She was careful, but she didn't recoil. She reached out and touched his neck.

Another unrecognizable person, except this time not just because he didn't know anyone anymore, but because the head of the very, *very* still body was covered in blood.

"He won't move!" the ranch hand yelled, not fully running up to the body on the ground. He looked from Rosalie to Duncan. "I kept shouting his name, and he won't move."

"What is your emergency?" Duncan heard vaguely from the speaker, jolting him back to his body—not some far-off place of shock. He lifted the phone to his ear. "Sorry. It seems… Someone's been hurt."

"We've already dispatched police and an ambulance. What kind of injury has the person sustained?"

"I'm not…sure." Duncan didn't want to look, but he couldn't help himself. "There's blood."

"Is the person conscious?" the dispatcher asked with a kind of detached calm Duncan envied. He felt jittery and outside his body. Because Duncan didn't think consciousness probably had much to do with anything right now. When Rosalie's gaze lifted to his and she shook her head slowly, he knew it didn't.

Duncan had to clear his throat to speak. "I don't think he's alive."

The dispatcher had him stay on the line and answer questions. Rosalie tried to calm the ranch hand who'd found them, but the kid just kept repeating the same information.

I called his name. He wouldn't move. Why won't he move?

As they waited, a few more ranch hands appeared, and Rosalie somehow managed to corral them all in the same area. She was about a foot shorter than all of them, but she had a kind of stature and calm in the face of all *this* that had every single person obeying her without question.

Duncan heard the blaring sirens before he saw the vehicles approaching. The police cruiser appeared first, followed by an ambulance. Both vehicles came to a stop on the drive, close to where they all stood.

Even as the paramedics rushed forward, Rosalie was walking past him, right for the uniformed cop who was striding toward the body. He couldn't make out exactly what she was saying, but her tone was confident. Authoritative.

And it was clear, the cop didn't like it. So Duncan moved over to her, not sure what he thought *he'd* do about anything. Only knowing he didn't like the scowl on the cop's face.

Rosalie didn't acknowledge his approach, but she must have noted it because she held out her hand. "Give me my phone, Duncan. I've got a phone call to make."

"You can go crying to your friends in the bureau, but that's not how this works," the cop told her. And not kindly.

"It's a free country, Stanley, which means it's how *I* work." She jammed a finger onto the screen of her phone and whirled away from the police officer.

Who was now studying him. "Name?" he demanded.

For a full minute, Duncan could only blink at the guy. "What?"

"Your name? You're not Natalie or Norman Kirk, so I need to know your name and reason for being on the property."

Duncan supposed he shouldn't be offended. Not everyone who knew his parents was going to know who he was, especially by sight, but the guy's tone *grated*. Everything about this guy grated.

"I am *a* Kirk. I'm Duncan Kirk, their son. So I'd say I know *Natalie and Norman* pretty well and have a pretty damn good reason for being on the property."

The guy looked taken aback for maybe a second, then went back to big-chested bluster. "Where are your parents then?"

"Mom's running errands." But he wasn't sure where his Dad was. With her? Somewhere on the property? But if he was around, shouldn't he have heard the commotion and come running?

Duncan's entire body went cold. Oh *God*. What if…? The phone in his pocket buzzed just as the fear of something awful befalling Dad gripped him.

It was a text from his dad.

What the hell is going on up there?

Duncan thought his legs might fully give out, just from relief alone. We've got a situation. Come on up to the north gate. Then he shoved his phone in his pocket and tried to find his strength again.

"My dad is on his way," Duncan told the cop. Then, before the guy could ask any more questions, Duncan turned away from him. He felt weak-kneed from that bright bolt of terror.

So he walked until he didn't. Until he found Rosalie. She didn't look at him, but she began speaking, and he could only figure it was *to* him.

"I called a detective at Bent County. He's rounding up the coroner, though the paramedics hopefully already put that call in. I don't know why Stanley has to be such an ass about it." She scowled over her shoulder at the guy, who was now talking to the ranch hand who'd gotten them. "You said your mom's out running errands. You better give her a call. No doubt if *anyone* noticed emergency services turning into the ranch, they're already calling her to ask what happened."

Duncan swore inwardly. "Dad texted asking what was going on. I just told him to come on up."

She nodded. "Call your mom, or text her, if she'll read those. Tell her you're okay."

"Why wouldn't I be okay?"

Rosalie shrugged. "Small-town gossip isn't always *true* gossip, Ace. You should know that. Text your mom."

Duncan sighed. He didn't like taking orders from anyone, but particularly this slip of a woman who was only a little more than a stranger to him. But he still pulled his phone out of his pocket and texted his mom.

Come home. I'm okay. Before he hit Send, he quickly added that Dad was okay too, then slid the phone back in his pocket just as yet another car he didn't recognize came to a stop next to the police car and ambulance, followed by a truck.

A guy dressed far too nice for ranch work, with expensive sunglasses, got out of the car. A woman who looked vaguely familiar got out of the truck. The woman headed for the paramedics, while the man made a beeline for Rosalie.

He approached, surveyed Duncan with a flicker of recognition, but he didn't say anything about it. "How'd you get roped into this?" he said by way of greeting to Rosalie.

"Long story," Rosalie returned, shading her eyes against the quickly rising sun.

"Well, Bent County will take it from here." He held out a hand to Duncan. "Detective Copeland Beckett, Bent County Sheriff's Department."

Duncan shook the offered hand, still feeling fully out of his body. "Duncan Kirk."

"Yeah, I know."

"It's his parents' place," Rosalie explained. "By the way, I don't want Stanley on this case."

The detective sighed. "You don't have a say," he replied with a shrug. And then, as if he realized it was not in his best interest to fully piss her off, he added, "Besides, he won't be investigating. I will."

Rosalie let out a huff of a breath. But once the detective walked away, toward the possible *murder* scene, she muttered something that sounded suspiciously like "so will I."

Which eased some of Duncan's tension, whether it should or not.

ROSALIE HUNG AROUND while Copeland asked questions, poked around the murder scene, conferred with the coroner. No matter how many times Copeland tried to shoo her away, she stuck close. She observed, kept a tally of questions and answers, and a mental note of everything she overheard. Once she had some time, she'd sit down and write it all out while the information was still fresh.

Copeland Beckett was a fine enough detective. She trusted him to do his due diligence, even if some of the people involved were incompetent.

Xavier Stanley was at the top of *that* list.

But this was too close to the Young Ranch, and until Rosalie knew why someone had murdered this guy, she wasn't about to back off and let anyone else handle the case, even if she trusted them.

Until she knew why that guy was murdered, and by who, she was working this case.

The body was removed, evidence sealed and packed away, pictures taken.

Rosalie snuck a few of her own on her cell phone when Copeland and Deputy Stanley weren't looking.

When the coroner was making the move to leave, Rosalie sidled up to her. Gracie Cooper was older than her, so they hadn't gone to school together and didn't really know each other socially, but that never stopped Rosalie from trying to press an advantage.

"You'll share that report with me, right?"

Gracie let out a sigh, the long-suffering kind. "Rosalie. You know better."

"It's for a case."

"Uh-huh." Gracie glanced at Duncan, gave Rosalie a *look* that implied things Rosalie would *not* acknowledge. "Some case."

Rosalie scowled, but she didn't argue with Gracie because she knew all about protesting too much.

But she did find herself looking back at Duncan. He stood with his parents, was about two inches taller than his dad and a few more than his mom. All three were looking at Deputy Stanley, and if the scowl on Duncan's face was anything to go by, he didn't like what he was hearing.

Duncan had been out of his element for a bit there. Hard to blame him, though Rosalie would have if he hadn't snapped out of it once his parents arrived on the scene. She'd watched him very carefully put all his *what the hell* away behind a demeanor that was firm and authoritative. He didn't let Copeland start asking questions until he was sure his parents were ready. He hadn't let anyone run roughshod over them.

She didn't care for the fact that she respected it.

"No reason for you to still be here."

Rosalie looked at Copeland, who'd come to stand next to her. He was clearly about to leave too. "The Kirks are friends of mine."

"The parents or the baseball player?"

"Both, thank you very much."

"Small towns," Copeland muttered with some disgust. Because he was Mr. Big City Hotshot. Except he'd landed here and stayed. So far. "I'm headed back to the department to put some stuff together. Stay away from my murder scene."

She smiled at him, batted her eyelashes. "Well, of *course*, Detective."

Copeland muttered curses all the way to his car. But he said something to a uniformed deputy—*not* Stanley, thank God—and Rosalie knew he'd leave someone posted until they were sure they had all the evidence and pictures taken they needed.

But she could get access to anything she needed. If not through Copeland, then through Hart. Oh, his loyalty would be to the Bent County Sheriff's Department, but with the right familial pressure, she could get what she wanted.

With that knowledge tucked away, she walked across the yard to Duncan. He was standing alone now, his gaze on where the body had been. Caution tape now marked the spot, and a lone deputy who stood watch.

Duncan turned that dark gaze to her when she approached. He offered a wry smile.

"How are they holding up?" Rosalie asked, nodding at the house.

"Mom's…upset. Dad's…upset. I guess that's really all there is to say. They'll feel responsible because it happened on their property, even if it had nothing to do with them."

Rosalie's heart twisted. What a terrible thing. "Was it one of your cousins?"

Duncan shook his head. "No, I guess this was a friend of one of the second cousins. Had some trouble back in North Dakota, so came here to get his life straightened out with Owen. That's the cousin."

"Maybe trouble followed him?"

Duncan nodded. "Sounds like. Owen talked to your detective. I imagine they'll look into that."

Rosalie nodded. "Mind if I talk to Owen?"

Duncan studied her. "He's been through a lot, but… Well, I don't know that detective. And neither do my parents. But they know you. We trust you."

Odd that he included himself in that *we*. Odd that it should make her feel something flutter inside of her. Like pressure, when she didn't believe in pressure.

Because Rosalie Young always got her man. "Good, because I intend to look into this."

"Whatever the fee, I'll pay it."

Rosalie shook her head. "No need. My sister and my cousin live just across that access road. I'm working on this for my own peace of mind over their safety."

"What about you?"

"What do you mean 'what about me?'"

"You live there too. You should be safe too."

"Yeah…" She knew she wasn't invincible. And she knew Audra and Franny weren't weaklings. It was just…

She was the protector. Always had been. Always would be.

"And I thought you all were armed and knew how to shoot. Wasn't that the warning you gave me?"

She scowled at him. "Sure, but… Well, that's all true, but that doesn't mean I'm not going to worry about a murderer lurking about. I protect my own."

Duncan looked back at the house, where his parents had gone inside. His expression was deadly serious. "So do I." Then he turned that serious expression onto her, and that *fluttering* was back, with a full set of *jittering* to go along with it. "I'm no detective or investigator, but I want to help. I'm *going* to help."

"How?"

"You tell me."

Chapter Five

Duncan wouldn't say he'd caught Rosalie off guard with his intention to help, but she didn't have a quick answer for that. In fact, when she did speak, it was with a question of her own.

"Where'd all the ranch hands go?"

"The detective said they could go back to their bunks, but no one is supposed to leave the property. They'll be back in a few hours with more questions."

"More questions and search warrants, I imagine. They'll want to go through all the buildings. Bunks, stables, the house. I don't know how long it'll take Gracie to determine time and cause of death."

"Gracie? Gracie Delaney?" He knew he'd recognized the woman. They'd gone to high school together. Though he couldn't remember much else about her besides the name and the vague look of *Delaney*—the family that had run Bent, more or less, back then.

"Gracie Cooper these days," Rosalie said offhandedly. "She's the coroner."

Coroner. Death. *Murder.* "I'm guessing the cause of death had something to do with the way his head was blown to hell."

Rosalie slid that pretty, blue gaze to him. "Noticed that, huh?"

"Hard not to." And yeah, it was going to haunt the hell out of him for a very long time, no matter how tough he tried to act.

"They'll want to find a murder weapon. It was a gunshot wound to the head, so they'll do what they can to identify a murder weapon, get search warrants and the like for anything that might match."

"You don't think one of the other ranch hands did it, do you?" The thought filled him with different kinds of dread for all sorts of reasons. The toll it would take on his parents. The danger they all might be in with a murderer running around.

What on earth had he come home to? At least he *was* home. This was the first time he was truly grateful for the timing. Because his parents would need him.

"Impossible to say just yet," Rosalie returned. She surveyed the crime scene, the rest of the ranch. "Let's go talk to Owen. See what he had to say about his friend."

Duncan hesitated. The poor kid had just stumbled upon his murdered friend and already answered a bunch of questions from the police. Should he let Rosalie pile on?

"Look, Duncan, you can either spare everyone's feelings or you can find the truth, but let me tell you from experience, you can't do both."

She said it kindly enough, but he felt *judged* all the same.

"Let's get the truth."

She nodded, then started striding away from the house. Since it was in the direction of the bunkhouse, he figured she knew where she was going. Though he wondered *why* she was so well-acquainted with the layout of the ranch. He followed her.

"Your shoulder holding up okay?" she asked pleasantly enough as they walked. She wasn't even looking at him, but he knew it wasn't a casual question. She'd noticed him wincing or something. And now she was slowing down, like he needed someone to slow down for him.

He focused on walking without showing any pain, and walked faster just to prove all was well. "I'm fine."

"Not what I asked."

He supposed it wasn't, and he didn't particularly care for her calling him out on it. So he grinned at her. "Worried about me, Red?"

She snorted, shook her head. "I'm worried about *murder*, Ace."

He blew out a breath. He was still trying to live in denial about *that*. "Yeah."

Once they got to the bunkhouse, Rosalie waited for him to knock. The door opened, and an older ranch hand stood in the opening, crossing his arms over his chest. Blocking the entrance.

Terry Boothe had been on the ranch since Duncan had been a kid, and Duncan was pretty sure he remembered Dad saying Terry was foreman now.

"Duncan," Terry greeted. He looked at Rosalie with suspicion and did *not* greet her.

"We just want to talk to Owen," Duncan said, hoping to offset some of the suspicion and distrust Terry was aiming Rosalie's way.

"Didn't he already—"

"I know he answered the detective's questions," Rosalie said, in a clear, polite tone that Duncan was sure he hadn't heard from her before. "And I'm sure he's broken up about this, but I have some questions that might help us figure this out that the cops aren't going to ask."

Terry's suspicion didn't lift. "What makes you better than the cops?"

"Not better. Different," Rosalie said, in that same even tone. "I'm a private investigator. Licensed, mind you. I've got rules and laws to follow, but I don't have a whole county with its bureaucracy breathing down my neck. The sooner we get to the bottom of this, the safer we all are. And Owen will be able to grieve fully."

Terry moved his hard gaze from Rosalie to Duncan. "Your parents okay with this?"

"Yeah," Duncan lied. He hadn't run it by them, but he couldn't imagine them having a problem with Rosalie helping. "Rosalie's a friend of the family. She just wants to help."

Terry grunted but he led them inside. The first room was the kitchen and dining area, open and wide, with a few tables. No one was in there right now, but Terry gestured them to a table. "I'll get him. You wait here."

They did just that, but Duncan noted that Rosalie was looking around the room like she was filing every detail away, like every dirty plate or can of soda was something that might answer a very simple question.

Who killed Hunter Villanova?

When Owen shuffled in, the poor guy was red-eyed and clearly overwrought. But he still walked over. Rosalie pushed a chair out for him, and he slumped into it.

Rosalie smiled at him, her look soft and reassuring. "Hi, Owen. My name's Rosalie Young. I live on the ranch just across the way. You probably know my sister, Audra, if you do anything with the agricultural society."

Owen seemed to struggle to take that all in, but eventually he nodded. "I know Audra."

"I don't want to take up too much of your time. I just want to ask some questions about what happened today."

Owen looked down at the table and nodded.

"I know some of what the detective already asked you, and I know it's frustrating to tell different people the same thing, so if you don't want to answer, you just go on and tell me that. No harm, no foul."

Owen blinked, looked up at her. Something like hope and trust flickered over his face. "Yeah, okay," he said, almost eagerly.

"Hunter and you came here from Bismarck?"

"Close enough. My mom and Mr. Kirk are related somehow. Mom said I had two choices. Get out of her house and make my own way or come on down here and work. I was getting in some trouble, and she was tired of it. Hunter…" He sucked in a breath, and it hitched. "I just don't understand what happened." He looked up at Rosalie, like maybe she could explain it to him.

"Can you tell me some things about him?" Rosalie asked gently. "Whatever you think might be important."

Duncan watched in fascination as Rosalie was…really, really sweet with Owen. She let him babble, and carefully would bring him back around to the main point—which seemed to be who would want to hurt Hunter, and what kind of people he was mixed up with. She didn't write anything down, like the detective had, but somehow Duncan knew she was filing every last point away.

Like the fact that Hunter had brothers who sold drugs. Which *seemed* like petty criminal nonsense, but he supposed with murder in the mix, you never knew.

When Owen started to get emotional again, big fat tears sliding down his cheeks, Rosalie rubbed her hand up and down the kid's back and offered to call his mom once she was done asking questions.

"Nah, Aunt Nat was going to do it for me." Owen looked up at Duncan. "I know he was trouble, but he really did want to get out of it. It was his idea to come with me. He wanted to get away from it."

Duncan nodded, wanting to reassure this guy he didn't even really know in some way. Just like Rosalie was doing. "I'm sure he did." He wasn't sure at all, but it seemed the right thing to say to this devastation.

"Thank you, Owen. I really appreciate it, and I'm going to do my best to help the detectives get to the bottom of it. They're going to keep asking you questions, and it's going to be hard, but you're going to get through it, because every answer is a chance for making sure whoever did this to Hunter pays."

Owen nodded as a few more tears fell. When Terry came back into the room, Rosalie gave Owen's shoulder a squeeze as she got up, then followed Duncan out of the bunkhouse and back into a shockingly sunny early afternoon.

They walked onto the pathway that led to the main house. Almost in tandem, they let out slow breaths and took deep ones of the summer sunshine.

"Hell, I feel old," Duncan muttered. "Back when I was twenty-two, I thought I was such an adult. Now I look at him and think what a kid he is. Shouldering all this."

"Yeah, we've all got things to shoulder. Life doesn't discriminate much, does it?"

"Guess not."

"Besides, you are old," she offered, with some forced cheer he knew was meant to be an attempt to lighten the mood.

And since he figured they both needed it, he went along with it. "Too old?" he replied, flashing a grin.

"Obviously," she replied, but she was smiling. Nah, not too old.

She sighed. "I'm going to head to my office, do some paperwork on this. When Detective Beckett comes back with search warrants and questions, I want you to pay attention. What the search warrants are for, what questions they ask. Record what you can if you don't have a good memory."

"I've got a good memory."

"Excellent. I'll be in touch." She started to march toward her truck, those short legs eating up the distance in quick time. A completely different person than she'd been back there at the bunkhouse.

Or was it different? Because she was taking on a case no one would pay her for. Out of concern for her sister, maybe, but she'd treated Owen like... Well, like he figured anyone would want to be treated in such an awful situation.

Duncan couldn't have managed that on his own.

"Rosalie."

She stopped, looked at him somewhat suspiciously.

He didn't know how this would have all gone down if she hadn't accidentally been here. Certainly not as smoothly. "I'm glad you were here."

There was just a *second* where she went completely still. An arrested expression crossed her face, then she shrugged and stalked away.

Duncan couldn't think about her reaction to that, or his. He had to go inside and deal with his parents.

Rosalie typed it all up. Her fingers moved *almost* as fast as her mind. She found in her years of working at Fool's Gold Investigations that people talked a lot more when you weren't taking notes or recording things. They gave information more freely when it felt like a conversation, like you cared about them as much as the case.

Owen Green was telling the truth. Rosalie knew that not because she believed she had some amazing ability to tell truth from lie, or that she didn't believe people could act. She'd learned her gut instincts *could* be fallible and *some* people didn't need a reason to lie—they just liked it.

But poor Owen was overwrought. Hurting. Grief was one of the few emotions she'd never seen someone fake well. When people were faking it, they just acted sad, or maybe they'd maneuver in a little anger. They cried a lot, yelled a lot. They didn't know that with grief always came a helpless undertone of shock, and guilt. No matter how old or young the deceased, no matter how peacefully they might have passed, grief and guilt held hands for those who'd loved the person they lost.

Rosalie muttered a foul curse under her breath, because she didn't want to be thinking about *grief.*

She focused on this case for the rest of the day. Well past dinnertime she was sending emails, making phone calls, and putting together what disparate details she could. Quinn popped in to say goodbye, and still Rosalie stayed at her desk and worked, only taking a quick break to tell Audra she wouldn't be home with pizza any time soon.

Later, she heard the faint sound of a knock and looked up, but she couldn't see the front door from where she sat in her office. Her gun was still holstered at her hip, so she put a hand to it as she stood and carefully moved to the doorway.

The front blinds were drawn for the night, but there was a little window at the door, and in the window, she saw a recognizable face.

Duncan.

Why that made her feel nervous she couldn't quite figure out. He was an easy enough guy to deal with. It was no doubt about work, so there was absolutely no reason for her heart to skip a beat.

She moved forward and opened the door. It was dark outside, though she saw a flicker of lightning in the distance and could smell the rain with it as well.

Which was the only reason she let him step inside, the threat of that storm in the distance.

So it was just her and Duncan alone in this old, finnicky building, with the lights dimmed for the night.

A strange tension wound itself into a tight ball in her chest. Not discomfort, not anything she fully recognized, and that left her feeling off-kilter. Unable to find her usual brash way through without her normal footing.

"Why are you here?" she asked, sounding far too grumpy and demanding.

He eyed her with some humor, which put her even more off balance. Who met rudeness with humor?

"Cops finally left. You said you wanted to know what they did and said."

"Yeah, I do, but you didn't have to come all the way out here."

He shrugged. "Mom's already planning the funeral—I guess Hunter's family wasn't interested. She had me run some errands for it, and I was in the area, so I thought I'd stop by and tell you. Be easier here, anyway."

Rosalie remembered then, with a clear detail she didn't want, how Natalie had stepped in and walked Mom through funeral preparations for Dad even as their entire foundation had crumbled around them.

The Kirks did what needed doing, and maybe she figured the hotshot baseball player who'd barely been home wouldn't follow suit, but clearly he did.

"We don't have to do it here if you're…" He trailed off. The humor didn't leave his expression. "Uncomfortable."

She barely resisted a scowl. "Why would I be uncomfortable?"

He gave a little shrug, still standing close to the doorway. "I'm a big guy. You're a small woman. It's late, and I assume we're in this building alone. I wouldn't blame you for feeling…intimidated."

She wasn't sure if he meant that to be a challenge, or if he was just an arrogant SOB. She patted the gun on her hip. "I'm armed." Because she wasn't *intimidated*. Rosalie Young didn't do intimidated. Never had.

But his amused smile stayed put. "Noted."

"And you're not that big," she continued. Childishly, she knew, but she just hadn't been able to stop herself. Because, of course he was *that* big. He had to be pushing six-five, and she was fairly certain there wasn't an ounce of body fat on that tall, muscular frame.

The way his mouth seemed to take its time unfurling into an upward curl, the way his dark eyes danced with humor, had unwanted and unfamiliar fireworks going off inside of her. Rosalie *hated* feeling knocked off her axis. She associated it with the aftermath of her father's death, and even if this was a kind of…an almost pleasant knocked-off-her-axis feeling, she still didn't trust it.

Or him for bringing out unfamiliar feelings.

"So run me through it," she said, brusquely turning away from him and marching back into her office.

He followed her into the room, took the seat across from her desk that she gestured to. When she looked at him again, the humor and smile had both melted away.

Back to murder and questions. She almost regretted it. Except this was her job and this was why he was even here.

"They came back with search warrants for the house and the bunks. They were really interested in gun safes and who owned what, the licenses everyone had. That sort of thing. Makes sense, I guess."

Rosalie nodded. That was about what she'd expected. "They'll be back once they know what kind of gun killed him. They'll compare what guns they first inventoried, make sure none mysteriously disappeared. They'll have more questions as they carefully and methodically build a case."

"Against who?"

"It'll depend on the guns. It'll depend on if they think they've found a motive. An investigation like this… It's all layers. They'll work hard, but unless it's easy answers, it'll be slow going."

Duncan clearly didn't like that answer, and Rosalie couldn't blame him.

He sat forward, balancing his elbows on his knees as he looked at her intently. "The thing is, if everything Owen said was true, Hunter was trying to get on the straight and narrow. He left the bad stuff behind in North Dakota. Why would it follow him all the way here? Why would it end in murder?"

"I've put some feelers out, as no doubt Detective Beckett has, to the authorities in North Dakota to see if we can get an idea of the trouble he'd been in, and who else was involved."

"What if it's nothing?"

"No point crossing that bridge 'til we come to it. First, we've got to find the nothing."

Duncan made a frustrated grunting sound. "I'm worried about my parents. Not just their safety, but the mental toll of all this. They were already worried about the missing cows, now this. If it drags on… I don't want it to drag on."

Rosalie's heart twisted at the genuine concern in his tone and on his face, but the cows…

Missing cows. Another unexplained bit of weirdness going on at the Kirk Ranch. "Could it be connected?" she wondered aloud, trying to work out *how.*

Duncan just stared at her for a full minute. "A murder and missing cows?"

"Neither make much sense, so maybe they don't make sense together. Did your parents or you tell the detective about the missing cows?"

Duncan was quiet a moment, clearly reaching back and remembering. He shook his head. "No, I don't suppose it occurred to any of us that the murder would have anything to do with something so…mundane."

"They should tell Detective Beckett. As soon as possible. Someone needs to bring it up. I'll corroborate you came to me before the murder. It'll help."

"Help what?"

"Duncan…" She hesitated, which was rare for her. She believed in being a straight shooter, and she left softening blows to people better suited to it. But the concern he felt for his parents was palpable and she didn't want to add to it.

It was the right thing to do, though. "If there's anything it looks like they're hiding, that's going to… It's going to draw attention to them."

"To… My *parents*?" The pure, unadulterated shock on his face made it clear that Duncan Kirk had never known a day of truly *unfair* in his life. "You can't be serious."

She wanted to resent his naivete, but… Well, Natalie and Norman Kirk were good, honest people. Why shouldn't he be offended on their behalf? "Duncan, you know your parents. I know your parents. The Bent County Sheriff's Department? They don't. At least, the lead detective doesn't. So he's going to treat them like facts on paper—and that might grate, but it's his job to do that. His job is facts."

Duncan stood up, somewhat abruptly. She thought maybe he was going to leave, but he just stood there, looking thunderous and...

Hot.

So not the time.

"If anyone so much as insinuates that my parents could have possibly had something to do with this murder—"

Rosalie stood, skirted the desk, and against her better judgment, reached out and put a hand on his arm.

He winced a little instead of finishing his sentence, and she realized her grip was on his bad arm.

She pulled her hand back. "Sorry," she muttered, feeling stupid for too many reasons to count. "Listen. You have to put your personal feelings away, okay? I know that's asking a lot, but if you get mad, then *you're* in the line of fire."

"So what?" he demanded. "I'll hire a passel of lawyers to drown their asses."

"Or," she returned evenly, "you could just tell the truth, Duncan. You could give the detectives everything they need to hopefully find a murderer. Put your pride aside, put your..." She hated to admit that she understood this was more than some rich guy's pride and pettiness. He wanted to protect his parents.

And that understanding made her softer than it should. "Put aside wanting to protect them. I get it. I really do. I'd protect my sister at any and all costs, but take it from someone who knows their way around a police investigation. If you take it upon yourself to protect—and keep the police at arm's length—you're only making everything worse."

He stood there, breathing a little hard, eyes blazing with a pointless anger she understood too well.

Damn it all to hell, the last thing she needed was to *understand him.*

"All right. I'll trust you on this, Rosalie." His gaze was hard, but she couldn't quite fight the shudder that jittered through her at the way he said her full name. "But you better be right."

Chapter Six

Duncan made it through the next few days on little more than caffeine and worry. His arm throbbed, because he never seemed to have anything to eat on hand to take his pain pill with. His head ached, both from too much caffeine and not enough sleep. And the worry that had tied its way around his entire body got tighter every day, not helping any with sleep or the ability to eat.

Mom took too much on her shoulders. Dad seemed like he was somehow disappearing in front of Duncan's very eyes. It reminded him too much of a time he only barely remembered, because he'd been five or six, when his grandmother had been sick and dying. The stress, worry, and grief had clung to the ranch then. As they did now.

He hated it. He didn't know what to do about it. Except volunteer for every errand, every ranch chore he could manage one-armed, more or less, and so on and so forth. Trying to take some of that weight away. *Any* of the weight.

Three days later, on a pretty afternoon, they held a small graveside funeral in the small cemetery in Sunrise for a young man almost no one had actually known.

The ceremony was small and depressing. Apparently poor Hunter Villanova didn't have much in the way of family. No one had wanted his remains, so Mom had taken it upon herself to secure him a plot and a stone here in Sunrise.

The entire group was made up of Duncan, his parents, Owen, and a handful of the ranch hands, including Terry. It would have just been Kirk Ranch people, but Rosalie was there.

With Audra and their cousin—Duncan couldn't quite remember her name—but he mostly just saw Rosalie and the way the afternoon sun glinted off her red hair, and the way a little breeze teased the tendrils around her face.

And maybe, most of all, the way she held herself. A little stiff. A lot formal. Like there was something she was bracing herself against. Not a weight, exactly, but something akin to one.

When the funeral ended, and Audra and the cousin drifted over to a section of the cemetery where the name *Young* seemed to dominate, Rosalie didn't follow. She stood a ways back, staring ahead at seemingly nothing without blinking.

It was then Duncan finally realized that she was likely bracing herself against grief. Because her dead were buried here.

But she didn't go pay them any respects, and that struck Duncan as...sad. Twisted something in him, so he stepped away from his parents—who were thanking the minister for handling the small, brief ceremony—to approach Rosalie.

"Afternoon," he offered in greeting, coming to stand next to her. He looked straight ahead too, trying to determine what she might be staring at.

"Audra thought it would do your mom some good if more than just Kirk Ranch came."

"She's right. It eased her heart some."

Rosalie sighed, and Duncan thought he should understand that sigh, but he couldn't quite reason it out. Or the almost wistful expression on Rosalie's face.

"Any news on the investigative front?" he asked, even though he figured he knew the answer. He doubted she'd keep information from him. They'd told Detective Beckett about the cows, as Rosalie had advised, but since then, nothing had really come to light.

"Not much," she said, and he could hear the frustration in her voice. "Anyone been back out to search the guns?"

Duncan shook his head. "Detective Beckett came out to talk to Terry yesterday, but I don't know what they talked about. I assume he told Dad, but Dad… He doesn't like to talk about it." And Duncan couldn't bring himself to press. "I told Beckett about the cows myself the day after I talked to you. He didn't have much interest in a connection."

Rosalie frowned a little at that, but she didn't offer anything else.

"I don't think anyone thinks we're in any immediate danger. It seems the consensus is that whatever Hunter had been mixed up in back in North Dakota followed him here. And if it had anything to do with cows, it was primarily coincidental."

"That would make the most sense, I suppose," Rosalie said, sounding less than convinced. Which Duncan had to admit, eased some small portion of the worry on his shoulders.

He looked over at his father. Pale. And in a strange kind of daze neither Duncan nor his mother seemed to know how to get through. "But Dad is taking it personally. Someone being hurt on his land."

Rosalie nodded slowly. "It's a desecration of something holy."

When Duncan stared at her, because that was exactly it and beautifully said, she shrugged in a jerking motion.

"To him," she said somewhat defensively.

"To him," Duncan agreed, surprised to find his throat a little tight. He understood that his parents lived in a tight-knit community. He tended to think of small-town life as one of gossip and a slow pace of running errands, but in the past few days, he'd been reminded of this.

It wasn't just community—nosiness and pettiness existed here just as assuredly as they did everywhere—but it was people who understood why some virtual stranger who had no family to bring him home might mean something to his parents.

Because the land was holy, and someone had desecrated it.

"I'm going to stop by the sheriff's department after this," Rosalie said into the heavy silence. "Rattle some cages." She offered him a pathetic attempt at a smile. "If there's anything of note, I'll let you know."

She started to move, but Duncan moved with her. He didn't know what he was going to do if he stayed here. He couldn't keep standing still, trying to hold everything together with just one working arm. He needed to…do something.

"Let me come with you," he said, on a whim, without thinking it through.

But when she looked at him with a kind of condescending refusal, the idea took root.

"Duncan," she said, shaking her head. "No."

He wasn't taking no for an answer. "Why not?"

"Because I'm a licensed private investigator off to do my job and you're…" She looked him up and down, no doubt weighing how mean she was going to be.

He kind of wished she'd be really mean. It'd give him something to fight against.

But in the end, she just said, "...some guy."

"Let me come with you," he insisted. He could follow her, either way, but it'd be better if they worked together. "I've got to *do* something."

He didn't know why it was that sentence that got through to her, but something about it had her relenting.

"Fine," she muttered. "You need a ride?"

He nodded. "I came over with my parents. But I'll let them know I'm hitching a ride with you. Unless you need to drop your sister off?"

Rosalie shook her head, even as her gaze darted over to where Audra stood next to a newer-looking stone.

"We came separately," Rosalie said firmly. She turned her back on Audra. "I'll meet you at my truck."

Duncan wasn't sure what was going on there, considering how close it seemed the sisters were when he'd dropped by their place. He made his way back to his parents so he could tell them he was heading into town. But before he made it to them, he took a little detour so he could see the name on the gravestone Audra had been standing next to before she and the cousin had moved over to talk to Mom.

Tim Young was carved clearly in stone.

Audra and Rosalie's dad.

Duncan glanced back at the parking lot, where Rosalie stood outside her truck, her back to the graves.

It wasn't any of his business, but he wondered what made one sister grieve and one sister turn her back on a memory.

Audra was still talking to his mother when he approached, but they both immediately stopped talking once he was in earshot and beamed similar smiles at him.

Why it felt suspicious, he couldn't fathom.

"I'm going to head into town for a bit. I'll be back at the ranch later," he told his mother.

"You didn't bring your truck."

"I'm going with Rosalie," he offered, somewhat reluctantly, because both Audra and Mom were already looking in Rosalie's direction. He didn't want to say it was about the investigation, because they were in a graveyard. He didn't want them thinking it was something else, because clearly they *were* thinking that.

Then he figured it would really annoy Rosalie if Mom and Audra thought that he and Rosalie were off doing something *together* together, so he just went with it. Let them think it. He sure hoped Audra asked Rosalie about it later today. Wished he could be there.

He said goodbye to his parents, then walked back to Rosalie. She climbed in the truck when she saw him coming, had the engine going by the time he managed to leverage himself up into the passenger seat.

"Here's the deal. I'm going to the station to see what I can find out that Detective Beckett doesn't want to tell me. So when we get into the detective's office, you let me do the talking. We'll use you as a potential distraction."

"How would I be a distraction?"

"Oh, I don't know. Hey, everyone, look, the famous baseball player is lurking about. Ask him for autographs while I take a tour of Beckett's desk."

He wriggled the hand hanging from his sling. "Not much on signing these days."

"Fine. We'll line the women up and you can smile at them. Maybe have a few swoon so Beckett has to do something."

"Are you calling my smile distracting, Rosalie?"

She rolled her eyes, but there was some humor to it. And that felt like such a relief, he wanted to lean into it.

"I think my mom has some suspicions. Audra too."

"Suspicions about what?" she asked, backing out of the cemetery parking lot.

"Why we're headed off together."

"You didn't tell them it was for the case?"

He looked at her, all feigned innocence that clearly irritated her. And amused him even more. "Should I have?"

She gave an injured sniff, focused on the road, and held the steering wheel just a touch too tight, if the white in her knuckles was anything to go by. "I'm sure they know," she said stiffly.

"Yeah," he replied. "I'm *sure*."

Her knuckles got even whiter as she drove.

ROSALIE STILL HADN'T decided how to handle Duncan. She figured the flirting was just for fun, or maybe even just part of his personality. Normally, that sort of thing didn't bother her any because it was usually *her* MO.

But something about Duncan really scrambled things up. Or maybe it was the *murder*, which he should care more about than scrambling her up.

Of course, she'd seen the way he'd looked at his parents. So full of worry. She saw the way the last several days hung on him, almost as much as it hung on his dad. Their color was off, and they both managed to look…gaunt.

Maybe that was the scramble. She didn't know this guy, not on any deeper level, but she saw things she recognized in him.

And she didn't *like* it. Any more than she liked his big frame taking up space in her truck. Or that pinched look on his face when they hit a bump and his arm in the sling bounced a little and clearly hurt him.

Or the fact it made her drive slower.

She pulled to a stop in the parking lot at the sheriff's department, then led Duncan inside.

She waved at the admin at the front desk, didn't bother to sign in because she knew Vicky wouldn't say anything to anyone about it, and made a beeline for the detective's office.

Copeland wasn't in it, and neither was the third Bent County detective, Laurel Delaney-Carson, but Hart was.

"Hart. How's it going?" Rosalie greeted, gesturing Duncan to follow her into the room.

"Going," the guy grumbled before glancing up. His gaze stopped on Duncan, clear recognition sweeping over him, but he didn't linger. He moved his eyes back to Rosalie. "Something I can do for you?"

"No, came to bother Copeland. Hart, this is Duncan Kirk. His parents own the ranch where the murder was. Duncan, Thomas Hart is a detective when he's not waylaid. Hey, look at that, you guys practically match." She pointed to both their slings when Thomas stood in greeting.

"I'd shake your hand, but as Rosalie so helpfully pointed out, I'm a bit stuck as of yet," Thomas said wryly.

"You're both old. You probably went to high school together," Rosalie offered, earning her scathing looks from both men. She smiled sweetly.

"I don't think we did. At least we didn't run in the same circles," Thomas said. "But it's nice to meet you, Duncan. Big fan."

"I don't suppose you blew your arm out throwing a ball," Duncan offered with some humor.

Hart smiled kindly. "Not quite."

"He got shot saving his wife's life," Rosalie said, because she knew somehow it would make them both uncomfortable. "Real hero stuff, our Thomas."

Before the conversation could continue, Copeland stormed into the office. His eyes were narrowed, and Rosalie figured he thought she was pumping Thomas for info. As if she'd do that here. She'd visit Vi if she wanted to secretly hound Thomas.

"I'm not giving you—either of you—any information you don't already have," Copeland said, pointing at Rosalie, then Duncan.

When Rosalie looked over at Hart, Copeland immediately stepped in her line of sight. "And none of that. You can't use your cousin's connection to Hart as some sort of leverage."

"Sure I can," Rosalie replied good-naturedly. "Vi marrying Thomas has been quite the boon for my business."

Copeland looked disgustedly at Hart, who shrugged. "I tell my wife everything. Don't plan to stop. Maybe you need yourself a wife, Cope."

"I'll chew my own arm off first," he muttered, returning his annoyed gaze to Rosalie. "I don't have anything for you."

"Maybe I have something for *you*." She didn't, of course, but he might slip up if he thought she did.

Copeland opened his mouth, no doubt to argue, but his eyes narrowed. He studied her. "You don't."

She lifted a shoulder. "Guess you'll never know."

His suspicious gaze turned to Duncan. "She doesn't."

But Duncan, clearly in the spirit of messing with Copeland, just shrugged.

"You don't have a lead on the murder weapon," Rosalie

said, wanting to poke at him until he gave something up. Since she really didn't have a gosh darn lead at the moment.

Copeland didn't react. So she kept poking.

"You don't have a hint of a suspect," she said, ticking the points off on her fingers. "You don't even know where to start looking for one."

"The victim was messed up with some dangerous stuff back in North Dakota," Copeland growled. "The most likely answer is something from his past caught up with him. We're looking into it. Along with all other leads that have been brought to us, including a rash of missing cattle."

But she saw it, in Copeland's thinly veiled frustration. In that blank way he delivered the information. He wasn't *hiding* anything.

"You really have nothing."

"We're investigating," he said stiffly.

But Rosalie felt deflated instead of victorious. She'd been certain Copeland would have caught wind of something she hadn't. He had more resources than she did, even if she could bend the rules a little bit.

And if he had all those resources, all these *detectives*, and he had nothing... It made her chest tighten. Like she was failing everyone.

She whirled out of the office and started marching back outside. It was just a setback. The cops had nothing, which meant she had to find something. She *had* to.

"It seems like my dad was right," Duncan said, following along easily enough.

"About what?"

"Some city detective doesn't belong here. No leads? What the hell is this?"

He didn't *sound* mad, but the take was an interesting one. She didn't blame Copeland's background on no leads, but… "You just moved back after living the high life in LA and you think you know more than a detective?"

"No, but I grew up here. I know ranching. That Detective Beckett probably doesn't know a bull from a cow. How would he know if anything Hunter was mixed up in had something to do with the ranch?"

Rosalie considered that. She didn't fully agree, but there were little true points hidden in his not fully correct one. And the thing was, Thomas might be from Bent, even Detective Delaney-Carson was *from* here, but they weren't ranchers. They might have an idea about things just from proximity, but they didn't have the full picture.

"You're right," she said, everything clicking into her head in the way she liked. In the way that prompted action, so she could follow one tiny little clue to the next.

"I am? Hey, say that again. I get the feeling I'm going to want to live off that admission for the next five years."

She ignored him, focused on the *point*. "They're detectives. They're not ranchers. Hart might be from here, but there's no ranching blood there. But me? I'm both. Sort of. Come on."

"Where are we going?"

"Back to your place, Ace."

She had a plan.

Chapter Seven

She drove like a mad woman, and though Duncan's heart leaped into his throat approximately four different times, he refused to show it. A woman like Rosalie would see clutching the door handle as a weakness.

Besides, he couldn't clutch a damn thing with his bad arm anyway.

She took a side entrance on the Young side of the property line, but cut over closer to his cabin where there was no real road or path.

He eyed her. "Been mapping out ways to come find me, Red?"

One side of her mouth curved up—amusement in spite of how badly he knew she didn't want to be amused by him. It eased something inside of him, this very simple human interaction that didn't have any weights to it. Even when his life had been baseball, every relationship had been full of weights—responsibility to his team, his manager, his agent. How he was representing the team, himself. His *brand*, as his agent liked to say.

And he loved his parents, with everything he was. There wasn't a weight there he didn't take on gladly and with enough humility to know the weights went both ways. Because when you loved people, you worried about them.

When people supported your dream, you wanted to do right by them in every way you could.

And he wanted to fix this stress for them, this hurt. This *desecration*. So that was a weight.

But with Rosalie, she was just…a friend. Helping him with a problem. And there were no weights.

For a minute, that felt just as disorienting as it did freeing. Especially when she pulled her truck to a stop in front of his cabin, then got out with a little hop and started marching right for the cabin. Up his porch, like she was coming inside with him and that…felt a little more like panic than ease.

He hurried up to the door, which he'd locked, so it wasn't like she could get inside. Still, he felt the need to bar the door with his body.

"I haven't unpacked yet."

She waved that away with the flick of a wrist. "I'm a slob. Won't bother me any." She gestured for the door. "Let me in or I'll assume you're hiding a murder weapon and a bunch of dead cows in there."

She smirked at him and since he genuinely didn't know what else to do, he let her inside. The curtains were drawn, so the room was dim. He could turn on the lights… He could do a lot of things, but exhaustion was poking at him. Pain—in his shoulder, his head. Since she wasn't explaining what was up, he took a seat on his couch. For just a moment, he closed his eyes and let out a long, slow breath.

"You're in pain." She said it like an accusation.

"You're not living if you're not in pain."

"That's the stupidest thing I've ever heard anyone say, and I deal with criminals on the regular."

When he opened his eyes, she was standing in front of him, hands on her hips. She was wearing a simple little black dress. It wasn't the right color for her at all, but he didn't mind the view of her legs. Which he took his time enjoying before meeting her gaze.

"It's the way of life for a professional pitcher. The older you get, the more it hurts."

She stared down at him, those violet eyes flashing with a restrained annoyance that never failed to amuse him. Or maybe *arouse* him was the more apt word, even if he was trying to ignore how much he liked being in her orbit. "Got any aspirin around here?" she demanded.

"For you or for me?"

She sighed at him as if he was a difficult toddler. "For you."

"I've got a pain pill I can take, but I need to eat something with it."

She marched right into his kitchen, poked around in the fridge and the little pantry. He almost told her to stop, that he'd handle it, but she just…moved around the space that he didn't think she'd ever been in and made him a sandwich without asking any questions. She filled a glass with water, brought both over, and set them on the coffee table in front of him. Then she put a little orange bottle there too.

"Eat. Take the pill. And learn this lesson pretty dang quick—you can't take care of the people in your life if you don't take care of yourself." She said this firmly, with enough conviction that he studied her.

"You do a lot of taking care?"

Her gaze skittered away from his. "I give it a shot every now and then. So here's what we're going to do." She was pacing in front of him now, but if he stopped eating, she'd stop, and glare at him until he did.

So he ate, while she laid it out.

"We're going to map it out, the missing cows. The cows

Audra found on our land last year all the way to the last one. Map it out by location. Mark it down by calendar. We're going to follow every last step from a ranching perspective and see if something jumps out and connects to a murder perspective."

He liked that it sounded like something, but it didn't sound like finding a murderer. "And if this has nothing to do with the murder?"

"We'll have figured out one mystery at least." She tapped her fingers on the table. "Listen, maybe this is the deadest of ends, but we're already at one. And so are the cops. If they won't follow this line, we have to. Because we've got ranch eyes, or at least I do."

"I've got ranch eyes," he muttered, feeling defensive because...yeah, he didn't have a clue. For the past fifteen years, he'd only been on this ranch on holidays. But there'd been a time—before high school, because even then his parents had let him focus on baseball—in the early part of his childhood when his life had been about setting him up for taking over the ranch someday.

He'd never...wanted that, but he'd been raised in it. So he wasn't ignorant. He wasn't going to let himself feel like he didn't belong right here. Like he didn't know more than those detectives who'd never dealt with calving or branding season and everything after and in between.

"Okay, so we use our inherent understanding," Rosalie said firmly, not arguing about his *ranch eyes*. "And maybe it's the wrong direction, but sometimes when you scale a brick wall, you get to the other side and realize it didn't lead you where you wanted to go at all. But other sometimes, that's an answer all on its own, or it leads you to a place you'd never have thought of otherwise. We need a map of the ranch."

Duncan nodded. "I can get my hands on a map."

"Then we need dates. More than just that list of cows your mom gave you. What was going on that day, who was working what jobs. Maybe you could talk to Terry about it. Or I can."

"I'll do it," Duncan said. "Not sure Terry's my biggest fan. Pretty sure he sees us both as outsiders, but he'll be more careful with you. If I get Mom behind me, he'll tell me everything."

"Okay. So I'll leave it up to you. Gather all that information, and we'll go from there. Tonight, I'll talk to Audra about everything she remembers when the cows ended up over at our place."

"Sure, I—" He was interrupted by a vibration in his pocket. He pulled out his phone and saw his agent's name. He could avoid it, but then he'd be distracted, and he still wanted to talk to Rosalie about Owen. "Can you wait here? Just a second. I have to take this, but... Just give me one second."

She eyed him suspiciously, but she nodded, so he walked deeper into the cabin and went into his bedroom. The last thing he wanted was Rosalie's eyes on him while he talked to Scott about baseball things.

ROSALIE WATCHED AS Duncan moved stiffly down the hall and into a room she suspected was his bedroom. He shut the door.

She'd never seen that look on his face before. A kind of hard-edged annoyance. Not quite as pissed off as she'd seen him get over things with the case. No, there was something too resigned about it.

Rosalie forced herself to survey the cabin instead of continuing to mine thoughts about Duncan's *facial* expressions. But there was something she had no compunction about mining.

Since he was occupied, Rosalie poked around his living room, which was indeed full of unpacked boxes. She'd been a private investigator too long not to take liberties when she had the opportunity. She nudged open a box in the corner, then just stared at it.

It was full of…trophies and awards. Somewhat haphazardly packed. None were wrapped up carefully, but a few sheets of bubble wrap were stuffed here and there. She didn't reach out and touch one, but she read the engraving on one that she could see. *Cy Young Award.*

It sent a strange wave of sympathy through her—which didn't make much sense, because he had an award she knew was incredibly important and amazing in his sport. He was loaded. He had gone out into the world and lived his dream. So why should she feel any sympathy for that, even if it had ended on a sour note?

But he'd been at the top of his game. A bona fide star. Now he was back in Wyoming and in constant pain, it seemed. With missing cows, murders, and worry about his parents.

And that was the foundation of where any sympathy came from. She could see it on his face, the way he wasn't taking care of himself. He worried far more about his parents than about his old awards, or life, or even his pain.

He'd been going around today hurting, all because he hadn't taken the time to eat something and take a pain pill.

She was just soft enough that she couldn't quite harden her heart against that. Which didn't seem fair at all.

"Did it ever occur to you some of that might be private?"

Rosalie refused to jump or startle. She glanced over at

him and smiled, not bothering to close the box. "Of course it occurred to me. That's why I looked."

Maybe she expected him to be angry about it. Maybe she hadn't really considered his reaction. But she sure wasn't prepared for that grin of his, and the way it shot through her like fireworks.

"You want to go through all my awards, Red?" he asked in that slick way he had that she really, *really* wished didn't affect her the way it did. "You'll be here all night."

Something about him saying *all night* poked holes in all her usual smarts. Because she should have let that go. Stepped back and away from the *danger, danger* of it all.

She didn't. "Well, if that's the most entertaining thing you can think of to do all night, no wonder you're back to living with your parents."

The air felt charged then. *All night* hanging around them like a storm that rolled in out of nowhere. Which just kept happening. Every time she was around him.

It's not going to stop.

No, it wasn't. Not when he moved closer, and she was not someone who retreated, even when she should. She stood her ground. She fought any threat head-on and with relish.

Except this one. She took a step back, and then another, until she found herself backed against a wall.

A place she had never found herself in all her life.

"That wasn't an invitation to prove yourself," she said, but she didn't sound like her normal, in-control, haughty self. She sounded winded.

Particularly when he stood in front of her, all tall and broad and so handsome it hurt.

He raised an eyebrow, leaned closer. "No?" he asked, reaching out. She thought he'd touch her face or something,

something she should stop him from doing. But he only smoothed a big hand over her hair.

Still that almost touch skittered through her like the sizzle of a lightning strike that hit close enough to worry about. "N-no."

"Did you just stutter?" he asked, too much amusement in his tone as he leaned close enough that she could feel his breath against her cheek. He smelled like clean, crisp winter. A hint of pine.

But she did *not* stutter. Wouldn't. Her scoffing laugh was high-pitched even to her own ears. But he was so *close*, and he was so damn *tall*. His eyes felt like magnets. Like entire solar systems that sucked her into their orbit.

She knew better than to be sucked in, than to get mixed up in anything that wasn't light and easy. Anything she wasn't in complete control of, and boy, was she not in control of this.

It was just…she could almost imagine it. His hands on her. His mouth on her. She could imagine it so well she was having a hard time reminding herself why she shouldn't let it happen. There was a reason.

Wasn't there?

"Rosalie." He said her name in a way she couldn't even describe. It was low, almost…pained. Like he felt even half the two polarizing things tearing her apart. She could *feel* his dark eyes searching her for some explanation, some answer, because for whatever reason there was this *question* between them, an unknowing she wanted an answer to.

And at the very same time, didn't want at all.

"Let's just see," he murmured. "Let me."

It wasn't a question. There was no answer she was supposed to have. It was almost an order, not that she ever took orders.

Ever.

But she *let him* anyway.

His mouth touched hers, the lightest, nothing touch. His eyes were still open and on hers. An answer to a question she didn't understand, because there were too many layers to it. To him. To her.

That would have been enough to have her stepping away, but it was like he sensed it. Her closing in and up, and he didn't let her. He deepened the kiss instead, bringing his hand up to cup her head and pull her in.

It was like being catapulted into a carnival ride. All spins, and dips, and a strange weightless joy. He didn't taste like cotton candy though. No, there was an edge to him, a danger at the periphery of all that summer sweetness.

And Rosalie had always been a little too intrigued by danger, the rush of it all. Because danger was simple, and temporary. It destroyed in little ways.

It was secrets, and time, and believing too much that destroyed in big ways. And that was what seemed to twist inside of her now. It was too big, too…something.

But the kiss was like a drug, even knowing it was a bad idea, she shouldn't do it, and it would be terrible for her, she sank into it, and him, and the sweet twining of want and need.

He eased his mouth away, his hand still cupped around her head, keeping her close. Too close. She blinked up at him, not altogether certain she was breathing. His dark, intense gaze just held hers, with a seriousness she couldn't *bear*.

What the hell was she doing?

"I have to go." She ducked out from his light grip, didn't look back. She had never been a coward in her life. Not once. But she needed to be one now. "You get all that information. Call me when you do."

Maybe he said her name, maybe she imagined it. But she got the hell out of Dodge while she could.

Chapter Eight

Though Duncan was tempted to follow her, he didn't. She'd looked…rattled, and he couldn't say he loved seeing rattled on steady, sturdy Rosalie Young.

He liked everything else he'd seen. The blush in her cheeks, her blue eyes shaded toward violet, that catch in her breath.

Did he know what he was doing? Hell no. He wasn't sure where to slot that kiss. He'd never once dipped his toes in complicated waters, because since he'd been twelve years old, and a coach had taken his parents aside after a Little League game and told them he had a *gift*, his one true love and passion had been baseball.

Sure, there'd been women, but there hadn't been relationships. He didn't have the time or inclination for complications, even in the offseason.

He didn't have to be in a relationship with Rosalie, or even know her all that well, to know there was no way to do casual in this world he found himself in.

So it was best that she'd run away.

But he looked around at his new life. Sans baseball—because just before this little interlude, he'd told Scott once more that he had no plans to attempt a comeback, take a coaching job, or anything remotely related to broadcasting.

He was terrified it would feel empty.

But he had his family now. His roots. His legacy. Things he'd let fall by the wayside for far too long.

So why should he balk at exploring something that might be deeper than a one-night stand in a hotel room?

When a knock sounded at the door, Duncan's eyebrows raised. Was she back? Now that would be something.

But it was not Rosalie.

"Mom." He glanced out at the yard. Would she have seen Rosalie rush out of here? Drive off? He didn't know how he felt about that. There was something like an echo of old teenage embarrassment, except she didn't say anything.

Which he was almost certain meant she hadn't seen anything. Mom didn't hesitate. She called him out. Always.

"Everything okay?" he asked, then shook his head. "Stupid question. Come on in."

Mom stepped inside. "Your dad is out running himself ragged. I thought maybe you could ride out and help him. I tried, but he's tired of me pecking at him. You two are excellent at sitting in silence."

He almost managed a smile at that.

"You don't have to go right away. He'll figure I sent you if we don't give him *some* alone time. But maybe in an hour or so you could hunt him down?"

He didn't ask why she'd come down to his cabin to ask that, because he could see as she moved restlessly around the front room, eyeing the boxes with a mix of frustration and zeal, that she was looking for things to do, to manage. That was how Mom dealt with stress.

"Sure. I'll track him down. Give him a run for his silent money," he said, hoping to make her smile.

She did, but it was small.

Because he couldn't joke or pester her out of this horrible reality they found themselves in. So maybe that was what he could do. Find answers.

"Rosalie wants to follow a theory about maybe this connecting to the missing cattle. I told her I could get a map of the ranch, and some more information about the times cattle have gone missing."

Mom frowned. "Of course," she said. "I'll get you a map. I… Don't tell your father, but I wrote down little details about the cows every time it happened. If I ever got him to go to the police, I thought it'd help. I'll give the notes to Rosalie. Or you."

"You've got enough on your plate. You get it to me, I can handle it."

Mom glanced at the door, something Duncan couldn't quite read in her expression. "You know, if you… You don't have to always be here, Duncan. You don't always have to be helping. Your father and I will muddle through."

He couldn't quite understand what she was trying to say, but he went for light and teasing. "Trying to get rid of me?"

"No, I just thought maybe you'd… Well, you don't need to focus on only this case, honey. You're home for good. You should…"

"I should what?"

"Settle in. Meet people. Connect."

He heard every silent word in between the words his mother spoke. *Grow up. Get married. Have kids.*

"Mom. Someone was murdered in your front yard just last week."

"Yes, and it's awful and tragic. But isn't that reminder enough? Life doesn't promise us anything. Might as well find some good in the midst of all that bad." She looked at the door again, considering. "Rosalie's a sweet girl."

Duncan snorted. *Sweet?* No, that was not what Rosalie

was. But she *was* something. "What's any of this got to do with Rosalie?"

She gave him a look then. "Come now, let's not play dumb. You've got your eyes all over her."

Duncan felt that old teenage embarrassment creep in, but he pushed it away. He wasn't going to be a coward just because this woman was his mother. "She's nice to look at."

Mom smiled at that. "She's nice, period. Had a rough go. She looks right back, you know."

His mouth curved in spite of himself. "I know."

She rolled her eyes, despairing of him and loving him in equal measures, as she always had. But her expression immediately sobered, her hands clasped and wringing the way they only did when she was really upset about something.

"I just… Something about that young man dying. What a waste. What a loss. Because there's nothing else he can do now. It's just over. I know you felt like losing baseball was…a death of sorts, and I'm not saying it isn't, or you can't grieve it. I just don't want you grieving it at the cost of life. Because you still have that."

He was rendered speechless for a moment. His mother wasn't afraid to wade in and say anything. Ever. But they didn't really have heart-to-hearts very often. He realized this really was stemming from poor Hunter's murder. Since it was, he tried to be honest with her, instead of doing what he wanted to do, which was fend her off.

"I'm not grieving it at the cost of anything, Mom." That was the truth of it, even if he hadn't really thought of it in those terms. "Maybe I was, but… I'm glad I came home, Mom. To help deal with this, but also because… It feels like life here."

"And I suppose you'll tell me Rosalie has nothing to do with that and I should butt out."

He studied her, knowing he shouldn't say it, but it'd get a smile out of her if he surprised her. "Maybe one of those things. I'll let you pick which one."

Rosalie got home late. She'd forgotten the pizza she'd promised to make up for last week. She was a mess. She'd be smart to go upstairs, take a long shower, and sleep.

She hunted for Audra instead. Found her in her little office, going over accounts, no doubt. Rosalie hesitated. She didn't want to interrupt Audra, who was already overworked, but...

Audra looked up.

"You got a few minutes?" Rosalie asked reluctantly.

"A few." Audra pursed her lips, studied Rosalie. "Have you eaten?"

"I'll scrounge up something in a minute. I've just got to finish this up. Can you tell me about when you found the Kirk cows on our property? Let me record it?"

"Okay." Audra leaned back in her chair, closed her eyes. "It was back in December. In fact..." She trailed off, got up, and went over to her sturdy stack of filing cabinets. She opened one, pulled out a little top spiral notebook. She hummed to herself as she flipped through the pages. "'December fourteenth. I found three of Norman Kirk's cattle in the east pasture. Returned by nightfall.'"

"Do you remember anything else?"

"We couldn't figure out how they'd gotten over to my place. I helped him and his foreman, and a couple of his hands, search fence line. Tried to retrace their path. It didn't make any sense, but poor Norman was distracted. That was around the time Duncan was having his second surgery, and I know they were just worried sick about him refusing to let them come down to California."

Rosalie tried to remember it, but she didn't really. She didn't pay attention to the ranch, and as nice as the Kirks were, she hadn't paid attention to them. She remembered the story Audra had brought home vaguely because she tended to file mysteries away.

But she hadn't thought about how that affected anyone. Not the Kirks, who were already dealing with worry about their injured son. Not Audra and how much she had on her plate, not just at their ranch, but at the agricultural society, and with neighbors.

Not the neighbor who'd had his whole life upended by some tendons snapping.

She refused to feel sorry for a millionaire who'd achieved his dreams, except she couldn't seem to help herself. What would it be like to devote your entire life to something that you always knew would end? Then it ended, not because of any choice you made, but because of bad luck?

"Rosalie. You aren't paying any attention."

Rosalie blinked back to where she was, what she *should* be thinking about. "Of course I am." Besides, it didn't matter if she'd been thinking of something else, because she was recording what Audra was saying. She could go over it in detail a million times.

"What's up with you?" Audra demanded.

"Nothing."

"Nothing?"

"Nothing."

Audra rolled her eyes. "The minute I mentioned Duncan, you went somewhere else."

She could lie to her sister. It wouldn't be the first time. She wanted to lie. She *planned* to lie, but when she opened her mouth the truth just sort of escaped. "Duncan…kissed me."

Audra beamed at her, all smiles and excitement. "That's fantastic."

"Why the hell would it be fantastic?" Rosalie demanded. "He shouldn't have done it, and I have no plans to repeat it."

Audra's expression fell. Then her eyebrows drew together and she leaned forward, and almost on a whisper, asked, "Was it bad?"

"Of course it wasn't *bad*. My God. He's handsome as a devil and knows it." And apparently knew other things. Like how to make a kiss twist and linger. So that even hours later, steeped in work, and worry, and exhaustion, it still felt like her lips were someone else's.

"Rosalie… There's nothing wrong with…" Audra sighed heavily. "Duncan's a nice guy from a nice family who seems to have an interest in you. You've got to stop pushing guys away just because…"

"Just because our father was a lying, cheating bastard?" Rosalie supplied for Audra. "Weirdly, that doesn't endear me to the gender as a whole."

"Dad was one guy," Audra said, almost defensively. Because she still dreamed of wedding days and happily-ever-afters, even though she kept herself on this stupid ranch, working too hard, giving too much to everyone but herself.

Rosalie looked at her sister then, wondering if after all these years she could actually get Audra to understand. It wasn't just what Dad had done… "You never saw him the way I did." Audra hadn't worshipped their father. *She'd* seen his shortcomings. Rosalie used to think Audra was just being mean, but she understood now. "And I'm glad you have sense when it comes to that sort of thing, but *I* clearly don't."

"Oh, honey." Audra reached out and Rosalie sidestepped

because she didn't want Audra's *sympathy*. "You don't really think that, do you?"

"It doesn't matter. I don't want that stuff. Why don't *you* go kiss Duncan?"

For a moment Audra was so still, so quiet. "Is that what you want?"

The thought of Duncan putting his hands on Audra made her want to crumble into dust. She *hated* the stab of jealousy, hated everything about this.

"There is nothing wrong with liking him," Audra said gently, when Rosalie couldn't manage a response.

"There is. And I don't. He's hot, sure, but so what? I'm a grown woman with a job to do. So that's what I'm going to go do." She moved to leave, but Audra blocked her way.

"We need to talk about Dad. And Mom, for that matter."

They had been avoiding this conversation for three years. Rosalie didn't know why Audra wanted to rehash it now, but Rosalie wasn't about to do it. Certainly not because of Duncan Kirk, of all things. "I don't have time, Audra."

"You do. If you're blaming yourself for thinking better of Dad than I did, then we need to have a talk. A real talk."

Rosalie's phone beeped. She had a text message. Even though Audra was scowling at her, Rosalie read it. Her heart rate picked up. "I've got to go." She nudged Audra out of the way.

"Rosalie."

"Duncan just texted me. The cops are at his parents' house, seizing a gun. I have to go."

Chapter Nine

"You're not taking anything before we get a lawyer," Duncan said, or maybe he'd yelled it. Panic was like a living thing inside of him, inside his parents' cozy living room. The front door was open, and two uniformed cops stood on the other side of the storm door on the porch behind Detective Whoever. The one Rosalie wasn't related to by marriage.

"We have a search warrant, Mr. Kirk," the detective said with a disdainful look at Duncan, like he was falling into every rich-guy stereotype, and maybe he was.

He didn't care.

When headlights cut across the drive, everyone turned to watch the approaching truck. Duncan didn't miss the way the detective and deputies' hands fell to their weapons. Then released them when Rosalie hopped out in the yellow glow of the porch light.

Detective Beckett looked back at Duncan with a hard expression. "Last time I checked, she wasn't a lawyer."

But Duncan didn't have to respond, because Rosalie was shouldering her way past the two cops on the porch. She opened the storm door herself and stepped into the living room, glaring at the detective.

"Come on, Copeland. You can't be serious."

"Can. Am. Look, if everyone is innocent, then it doesn't matter. The tests will prove it. We have a search warrant. I'm trying to be nice here, but I don't have to be."

"The ballistics report came back?"

"Isn't that the kind of thing you should already illegally know, Rosalie?"

"There isn't anything illegal about my investigations, Copeland. If there was, no doubt you'd arrest me. Now, you've gotten the report back, and matched it to a gun the Kirks own? Is that right? Because if you came out and told them what was going on, things would go a lot smoother."

"I can have you removed, Rosalie."

She ignored him and turned to face Duncan's parents. Who looked pale and anxious.

"There's nothing wrong with letting the police do their job," she told them gently. "Even if it's a waste of everyone's time," Rosalie continued, smiling at his parents.

She didn't *look* at Detective Beckett, who was scowling at her, but Duncan figured she knew it was happening.

"I'll get the key," Mom said quietly.

"I'm afraid I'll have to go with you, ma'am."

"Like hell—"

"Stand down, boys," Rosalie said cheerfully to both Duncan and Dad, because apparently they'd been saying the same thing. "You two sit. I'll handle it." She gave Duncan a pointed look, and realized she was putting on that cheerful, breezy demeanor for his parents' sake.

And since she was, he nodded. Then he nudged his dad into a seat at the kitchen table while Rosalie, Mom, and the detective moved deeper in the house to get to the gun safe.

"What the hell is happening?" Dad muttered, looking at his hands. They suddenly looked old to Duncan, and his heart lurched. The amount of anxiety and stress this was putting on his parents was too much. It just wasn't fair.

"I don't know, Dad, but Rosalie will get to the bottom of it."

Dad took in a deep breath, then let it out. "She's a smart girl," Dad said, squeezing his hands into fists then spreading his fingers wide. "I don't trust that detective, but I trust Rosalie."

Duncan nodded. On that, they agreed. But when Mom, Rosalie, and Detective Beckett reappeared, Duncan's entire body went ice-cold.

The detective carried two guns. He wore gloves, and instructed one of the deputies on the porch to put his on before he handed the guns to him. Duncan could only stare in utter shock.

When he looked back at Rosalie, her expression was grave, but she immediately wiped that away into something more blank once she knew he was looking.

Which scared the hell out of him.

"Who has access to this gun cabinet, Mr. Kirk?" the detective asked.

"Myself."

"And?"

Dad shrugged, looked away. Not because he wanted to lie, Duncan knew, but because he wanted to *protect*.

Since Duncan wasn't about to let Dad take the fall for *anything*, he continued the list. "Me."

"Duncan," Mom said disgustedly. "You couldn't find the key if I handed it to you on a silver platter."

"I know where you keep the key," he insisted. Lying, but he'd lie. He'd do whatever.

"Prove it, Ace," Rosalie said. Why the hell was she putting him on the spot? Why wouldn't anyone let him…protect? He remembered what Rosalie had said about letting the cops do their job.

It didn't soothe him any, but he figured... Well, like Dad said. Rosalie was smart. They trusted Rosalie. He tried to breathe through the anxiety riding high in his chest, and though he was going to try to move forward with cooperation, he scowled at Rosalie, then his mother, for not letting him tell a little protective lie. "Okay, I don't know where it is, but I could have asked. I could have found it. Anyone could have—"

"You didn't," Mom said firmly. Then she turned to the detective. "There are two keys. Norman and I keep one at the house, and only we know where. The second key is with Terry Boothe, our foreman."

The detective looked at the uniformed officer behind him, the one without the guns, gave a nod. The guy took off. No doubt to round up Terry.

"Now, don't go harassing my boys in the middle of the night," Dad said, pushing to his feet and pointing at Detective Beckett. "That's not how things are done around here."

"That's how they're done in a murder investigation, Mr. Kirk. Two guns registered to you could be the murder weapon. We have a search warrant and the authority to confiscate them so tests can be done. We'll head down to talk to Mr. Boothe, then we'll be on our way. I know I don't have to repeat myself, but it'd be in everyone's best interest if they stayed put, if they cooperated with the deputies. We all want the same thing, don't we?"

Duncan figured his answer was *no*, because at the moment, he wanted Copeland Beckett to rot in hell. But even he knew he shouldn't voice that. Though it took biting his tongue not to.

"I'm going to be straight with you all. I could arrest you,

Mr. Kirk, or Mrs. Kirk, or both, if I had any reason to believe you'd be behind something like this, even without the
tests. But I don't see any motive, any reason. *Yet.* So please,
if you really want answers, forget that I'm an outsider, drop
the small-town, circle-the-wagons, tight-lipped merry-go-
round, and let me do my *job.*"

His parents didn't say anything to that, and Duncan
couldn't really either. It didn't endear the detective to him
any, but the idea he *could* arrest his innocent parents, and
wasn't…*yet*… It was some kind of relief. Some kind of
hope that… That no matter what anything looked like, the
truth really was the goal.

But he still didn't like the guy.

"We'll be in touch," the detective said before pushing
out the door. He headed down to the bunkhouse to question Terry. And put the whole ranch up in arms.

But Duncan knew that if either of the guns they'd confiscated connected to the murder, it implicated someone
on this ranch.

IN THE WAKE of the police leaving, the silence was a heavy
weight that reminded Rosalie of times in her life she didn't
wish to revisit. Stress, worry, shock, and that horrible *what
do we do.* So she took charge of the situation.

"Mr. Kirk, it would be quite a feat for someone to sneak
into your house, steal your gun, kill that boy, then put it
back," Rosalie told him. "Not impossible, but quite a feat. If
it comes back that one of those guns is the murder weapon,
I don't think the suspicion would be on you. It'd be someone who works for you."

"No one who works for me would do such a thing," Norman said, offended.

But Rosalie watched as Duncan shared a look with his

mother. Maybe they didn't love the idea that one of the ranch hands could *murder*, but they both knew Norman was too kind when it came to all those troubled distant cousins.

Rosalie didn't argue with him though. No point to it. She had researched all of them. There weren't any violent offenders, but she'd keep digging on each of them. "You've got a detective bureau and an investigator looking into it. I know I can't tell you not to worry, but I'm determined to help get to the bottom of this. Keep cooperating with Detective Beckett. As much as his bedside demeanor leaves something to be desired, he's right. Shutting him out just because he doesn't know us won't help. But I'm not going to let what he doesn't know—about Bent County, about ranching, about you all—affect you. That's a promise."

Mrs. Kirk rose, walked over to her, and enveloped her into a warm, motherly hug that smelled like cinnamon and felt like an old memory Rosalie certainly wasn't going to indulge in right now.

She awkwardly patted Mrs. Kirk's back before the woman released her. "Thank you, Rosalie." Her eyes were shiny, but she didn't cry. She turned to her husband. "Come on, Norman. Let's get some sleep. Duncan can lock up."

Rosalie watched them go, wishing there was more she could do. Wishing she could see something in this case that Copeland and Bent County didn't see. *Wishing* for faster, better answers, and maybe a time machine to just erase this.

But those were never useful thoughts or feelings.

"Thanks for coming," Duncan said.

She should say "you're welcome" and leave it at that, but… Well, sometimes she really couldn't help herself. "You've got to stop trying to play hero, Duncan. We're all on the same side."

His expression hardened. She looked away before she

cataloged too many things about the way his eyes darkened, or lines bracketed his mouth, or how her stomach did an entire gymnastics routine if she spent too long looking at him—whether he was smiling or scowling.

"Not if they let my parents think, for even a second, they might be implicated."

Her response was a little curt, and not because he deserved it, but because she didn't like the thing going on in her chest. "They're adults. It sucks, but they can handle it."

"*I'll* handle it."

She rolled her eyes. *Men.* "Are you always this frustrating?"

"Yes," he said firmly. But his demeanor changed. Lightened. "Come on. I'll walk you to your car. And I can already tell you're opening your mouth to say I don't need to, but if you say that, I'm going to assume you're scared to be alone with me."

"Nothing about you scares me, Ace." *Wow, Rosalie, could you lie any harder?* Since she recognized the lie, instead of settling into the denial like she wanted to, she walked for the door. And she didn't argue when he followed, when he walked her out to her truck. She just marched on ahead and told herself that once she was in her driver's seat, she'd feel in charge again.

Except, when she turned to give him one last warning about trying to protect his parents, she was effectively caged against her truck. He wasn't *touching* her, and she wouldn't need to even use self-defense to get out of this, but she stayed there all the same. Back to the truck door. Front to him. A *him* who was far too close.

"What do you think you're doing?" she demanded, glaring up at him. But that was the only weapon she wielded.

She didn't try to push him away. She didn't draw attention to the gun at her hip. She just glared.

While Duncan's small, tired smile curved up. "Looking."

"Well, stop."

"All right." But he didn't back off. Instead, he lowered his mouth to hers. Not like back at his cabin. With a pause, with a softness.

No, he swooped in. Just like… Like they were doing this thing. Like he had any right to just lean in and kiss her. Like his mouth was made for hers and everything she ever thought she knew about how to handle a guy was a joke, because there was no handling *this*. This twisted-up, dizzying feeling he brought out in her.

But *God*, he was good at it. All those arguments she held very near and dear to her heart seemed to turn to ash and scatter on the wind. All that self-control she was so proud of disappeared somewhere.

A kiss wasn't a vow, she told herself as she kissed him back. It was just a kiss, and kisses were fun, she reminded herself, even as his arms came around her and pulled her flush with the long, muscular frame of his body…one arm holding on a little tighter than the other.

And because it did, because she wanted to fix that injury for him in spite of herself, she wrapped her own arms around his neck and held on tight with her two good arms.

His big hand smoothed down her back, and this kiss eased, ended. But he pressed another one to the corner of her mouth, then her jaw, her neck. Soft, almost reverent, and that slowdown had alarm bells trying to sound in her head.

Her heart was vibrating in her chest. She wasn't sure she could walk straight if she had to. She didn't understand what was happening to her, but she knew she couldn't trust it. She knew she had to hate it.

"I'm not starting anything with you, Duncan." Because that was what this all felt like. A start. And just the *thought* had tears she refused to shed springing to her eyes. Almost like she was painfully, wistfully, desperate for some kind of *start* with him.

Not in the cards.

Except he made a noncommittal kind of sound, then pressed his mouth to hers again. Soft, a little needy, like a man seeking comfort. And she might have resisted that, she told herself she would have had that strength because needy was dangerous, but then he spoke against her mouth. "Thank you for coming."

"You already said that," she returned, not pulling away from him. The fact that he kept saying it warmed her in ways it shouldn't. In ways she didn't like. Didn't *want* to like.

"I really mean it," he murmured, still there against her mouth. Like they were fused, connected, *right*.

"I have to go." But she wasn't pushing him away, was she? No, she let his arm stay wound around her, she let his mouth stay on hers.

"You don't *have* to go."

Tempting. Damn it, why was he so tempting? "You want me to solve a murder or you want to talk me into bed?"

"Why can't it be both?"

She shouldn't laugh, but she couldn't help herself. Nothing was funny about this, and she wanted to accuse him of not taking it seriously. But she'd seen him in there with his parents, how he tried to shield them.

She'd said she protected her own and he'd said "so do I" like it was a vow.

But she wasn't his, and she wasn't about to fool herself into thinking there was any way for this to work out. She gave him a nudge, and he went. She refused to acknowledge that his expression, only dimly illuminated by his parents' porch light, was one of amusement as he let himself be nudged away.

But he didn't let her go without a parting shot.

"I've got a thing for you, Rosalie."

"Keep that *thing* in your pants," she muttered, even knowing that's not what he meant. She turned her back to him so she could unlock her truck and jerk her door open.

"You can play that game if you've got to, but I don't."

She heard it, that hard edge of warning in his tone. She didn't take the warning. "Last I checked, you played a game for a living."

"Past tense, as you well know. I'm home now. New life. New…everything. And I'm happy to be patient, to focus on murder investigations. For a time. But only a time."

"You'll be sorely disappointed."

"Why, Rosalie Young, what makes you think I'd be disappointed in a thing about you?" He said it with a grin, but his eyes were serious. He backed away, then slowly turned, and headed back to his parents' house.

Leaving her there, blinking after him. Rocked to her core.

Because of course she wasn't disappointing. That wasn't what she'd meant.

But it felt like he'd lanced her through just the same.

Stay away from this man, Rosalie. Far, far away.

She repeated that mantra all the way home.

Chapter Ten

The next morning, Duncan blearily drank his coffee while looking over everything Mom had given him. A map of the property with the cow losses marked. Her copied recollections about what had happened each day.

He couldn't say he'd slept well. He was churned up about too many things. Murder and that kiss…*kisses* with Rosalie. Which he'd much rather concern himself with, but he couldn't deny the murder was more pressing.

He sighed.

Last night, he'd considered staying up at the cabin with his parents, but figured the separation was good for all of them. Pretend things were normal, even when they weren't.

He had moments of worry but he couldn't think of a single reason his parents would be targets. Even if the murderer ended up being one of the ranch hands, Dad had been nothing but kind and giving. Mom too, even with her reservations about some of them.

Besides, he'd hired a security business in Bent to come out and install a security system today. He knew it didn't solve *every* threat, but it would ease his mind considerably at night. He'd set the alarm himself every night if he had to.

He ate some breakfast, then headed up to the main house and met the installers. Mom would be volunteering at the

Sunrise library until dinnertime. Dad would be out working until about then too. So Duncan had a few hours to get into town and deal with Rosalie and the case before he had to be back to explain the new system to them. And figure out whatever tricks in the book he had to pull out to make sure they used it. Mostly guilt.

With that sorted, he packed up what Mom had given him about the missing cattle and drove out to Wilde to hand the information over to Rosalie.

She'd tell him he didn't need to bring it up to her. She'd be frustrated with him in her office space.

Which made it all the more enticing. It was good to move. Good to do. Good to think about something that felt like life instead of death. Just like Mom had said.

Duncan parked in front of the old building. Since it was during office hours, this time the front door was unlocked. He pulled it open and step into the cozy lobby.

A young girl, middle or high school—he wasn't good with ages—jumped to her feet from a chair. He noted there was a softball glove clutched in her hands and eager excitement in her eyes. "Hi," she greeted exuberantly.

The woman who'd been here the first day he'd come in strode out from back in the office somewhere and rolled her eyes. "Down girl," she muttered at the teen. "Sorry about her. My niece. Once she heard you'd been in the office, she wouldn't stop hounding me. I told her she could pick one day to come in, and if you happened to show up, she could pester you." The woman looked dolefully at the teen, then back at Duncan. "You picked the wrong day."

"I'm Sarabeth," the girl interjected.

"Hi, Sarabeth. I'm Duncan."

"I know. Duncan Kirk. I know all your stats. Want me to recite them?"

"Uh, no. I'm…good." Back in LA, he'd been used to this kind of thing. Had dealing with fans, especially eager kids, down to a science. But something about being home, about the way Rosalie's boss was studying him, made his usual ease with excited kids less than *easy*.

"You, uh, play softball?" he asked, gesturing at the glove she was clutching.

Her face fell a little at that. "I play softball *and* baseball," she said, not *quite* with a sneer, but close. Eagerness seemed to take over any affront though. "Fall's for softball. Baseball is in the spring—I'm the first and only girl on the Bent County High School baseball team. I pitched a shutout last week. Struck out eight." Her grin was one of easy teenage pride—he recognized it, felt some echo of himself in it. "All boys," she said smugly.

"How'd they take that?"

She grinned at him, hazel eyes alight with mischief. "Like babies." She practically bounced on her heels. "We're going to our conference playoffs this week. I'm starting again. Will you sign my glove for good luck?" She held it out to him.

He took it. It was almost like rote muscle memory. Take the glove. Sign the glove. Smile and compliment.

But his shoulder was in its sling, and it twinged in pain as he tried to hold the weight of the glove in it. He couldn't do the usual, because… "You did see my arm explode on national television, right?"

"Sure. But I'm not old yet. I figure it'll be lucky 'til I am."

He laughed in spite of himself, met Quinn's amused gaze as she tried to hide her own laugh. Quinn handed him a marker.

He balanced the glove as best he could with his good

arm, fought back a wince as he signed the heel of her glove and handed it back to her. "Mow 'em down, kid."

"I will. Thanks. Thanks a lot! It's tomorrow night at Bent County High School at seven o'clock if you want to come."

"Hell, Sarabeth. I'm taking you home, you menace. Rosalie!" she called out. "Going on my lunch. I'll be back."

Rosalie appeared in her office doorway. He watched as her quick gaze took in Sarabeth, the glove, him. "Sure, Quinn. I'll hold down the fort." She nodded at him. "Duncan."

She looked wary, so he grinned at her.

She didn't grin back. She was guarded again, trying to hold him off with cool indifference. But he saw the faint hint of pink at her cheeks. There was no way she wasn't reliving—at least a little bit—that kiss from last night.

And that put him in quite the good mood.

ROSALIE DIDN'T WANT to have Duncan in the close quarters of her office, cowardice or not. Especially the way he was grinning at her, like he could read her mind. Or her memories.

She still hadn't been able to shake that damn kiss. *Kisses.*

So she stayed where she was, leaning against her office doorframe, while Quinn and Sarabeth said their goodbyes and left.

"I'd apologize for them, but… Sarabeth's a special kid. She's been through a lot. Deserves a thrill of a lifetime, no matter how misguided she is for thinking your signature is a thrill."

Duncan, of course, didn't take offense to her little jab. His grin didn't die. He just kept *looking* at her and moving toward her. Normally, she'd refuse to retreat, but she had a bad feeling if she let him get within touching distance, she wouldn't have the presence of mind to stop whatever he would do.

So she turned her back to him, moved into her office, and sat down in her chair behind her desk. To create a nice boundary between them. She refused to acknowledge the amusement on his expression as he took the seat across from her desk.

"I've got what I call character sketches of all the ranch hands," she said, jumping right into business. "Terry, obviously, is going to garner the most attention from the detectives since he had a key. So I want to let the detectives handle that, and I'll put my attention elsewhere. Cover all our bases."

Duncan nodded. "I've got the map. Mom's recollection of what happened on the days the cows went missing." He put the folder she hadn't seen him carrying on her desk.

Rosalie opened it. She was most curious about the map. She wanted to picture everything, visually. Get a sense of the space of the whole timeline of events. She spread out the map on her desk, then stood so she could see it better.

"The red circle is the general area they think the cows disappeared from. *Xs* are where they found dead cattle— just the one time. Hash marks are where the rest of the herd was, approximately. It's dated here, and the dates match up to Mom's recollections."

Rosalie didn't want to look at the recollections or dates just yet. First, she wanted this sense of place. The missing cattle didn't cluster. There was the first incident—the missing cows found on the Young Ranch.

She wouldn't call what she noticed a pattern exactly, but it was movement.

She pointed it out to Duncan. "They move. Slowly. Closer and closer to the west side of the ranch. First, you had three end up on our property." She put her finger on the map, slid it over. "Then you had two disappear, and a cow found dead here. Seemingly two different problems, but maybe not." She moved her finger again. "One disappears here. Two weeks before the murder."

"Doesn't this kind of follow the pathway you drove me on the other day?"

Rosalie nodded. She didn't like that. Didn't like the proximity to Audra and Franny and their own herd.

Duncan pointed to a spot on the map. The pasture where Owen had found Hunter.

"If you include the murder, it follows the movement."

"But not the path," Rosalie murmured, considering all the different angles.

"No, but there's a cut-through right here." He pointed again, slid his finger from that point to the pasture. "Or there was when I was a kid. I haven't paid close attention, but when I go back this afternoon, I'll check it out. Back when I was a kid, we used it as a cut-through. Ranch hands, dogs, horses, whoever and whatever if we didn't want to take the service road around but needed to get up to the house."

"Or maybe, in this case, the pasture."

Duncan nodded grimly. "But what does it mean?"

"I'm not sure yet. I'll go through your mom's recollections. I might go over it with Audra too. How she got the cattle back to your dad." Rosalie had been avoiding Audra since last night, and wanted to continue to do so, but eventually she'd have to face her. Might as well be for work.

"In the meantime, I want you to go over these write-ups I put together on the other ranch hands besides Terry. Add your own interpretations, and ideally, your mom's. Unless it'll be too tough on her." She got out the papers she'd printed out earlier, stapled them together and handed them across the desk.

"No, she'll want to help. And she'll be able to give Dad's real opinions on them too—not just the no-one-would-murder one he gave the cops."

That was good. Rosalie didn't see any reason for it not to be a Kirk ranch hand, even *if* the guns confiscated weren't the murder weapons. Someone on that ranch had to have helped.

If she hadn't heard from someone at Bent County by dinner, she'd head down to the department and see what she could irritate out of Copeland. If that didn't work, maybe she'd stop by Vi's on the pretense of catching up and playing with Mags and see what she could pump out of Hart.

"You've been hard at work," Duncan said, skimming over what she'd put together about all the ranch hands.

She had indeed been hard at work, and not just to avoid all the things she was hoping to avoid. She didn't like the way this case nagged at her. Like there was a very clear piece she was missing, when, of course, nothing was clear, or Copeland and Bent County would have figured it out by now.

"Go out with me."

She didn't stiffen at those words, at the calm, casual way Duncan threw them out. She didn't let herself react outwardly. She just carefully raised her gaze to his. "We're working, Duncan."

This did not deter him. "I heard there's a hot-ticket, high-school baseball game tomorrow night at Bent County High."

That shocked her enough to forget about keeping her guard up. He wanted to go to Sarabeth's baseball game? "You want to take me to a high-school baseball game?"

"Sure. Why not? We'll see what that kid's got in the tank," he said, clearly referring to Sarabeth. "She seemed pretty sure of herself. Turns out, I like sure of herself."

It really was no wonder she liked him, because that simple summation of Sarabeth, and whatever interest he had—real or feigned—would make that kid's day, and that made Rosalie far too warm and fuzzy.

But she just couldn't…trust this. *Him*. What was she going to do? Go out with him? Sleep with him? Then what?

There was no *then what* in her future. Why couldn't he get that through his thick skull? Well, it probably wasn't his *skull* that was making his decisions, was it? And he'd been away enough to forget that small-town liaisons tended to bite you in the ass. If he really stayed, they were going to be neighbors for the rest of their lives.

"There's a murderer running around," she told him firmly. And ignored the fact she didn't say the simplest thing, which would have been no.

"You have the lamest excuses, Rosalie."

She didn't want to laugh. Damn it, it wasn't funny. But the sound bubbled up inside of her anyway.

He was grinning back, but then sobered some, in his eyes. "I set up a security system at the house this morning. Mom… Before the cops came out last night, she… Well, she's worried about so much. Murder at the center, but me in the fringes. It'd help, I think, if she thought I wasn't flinging myself into murder investigations like some kind of distraction."

"So you're only asking me out to keep your mom happy?"

"Sure, if that's what it takes to get you to say yes."

She didn't know what to say to that. She was torn between being insulted and that horrible, creeping warm feeling. It was terribly sweet, and she didn't want him to want to date her anyway. So why shouldn't it be about his mother?

Because it's not, and you know it's not.

"What security company did you use?" she asked, hoping maybe she could work her way around the entire subject. Hoping this somehow just…went away. Which had never been her MO in her entire life, but it felt like the only way to survive one very charming Duncan Kirk.

"Some company in Bent. Run by a Delaney."

"Cam Delaney. We used him ourselves at the ranch a few years back. Does good work. A security system can't cover a whole ranch, though."

"No. We talked about some solutions there, but I knew my parents would flip if they thought I was going overboard. I can get away with the house. Use guilt and all that, but the whole ranch? Dad'll put his foot down there. Until I wear him down. Hopefully we'll have everything solved quickly so I won't have to wear him down."

Rosalie wanted to smile at the fact Norman Kirk was the most quintessential kind of Wyoming rancher, but nothing about this felt *quick* enough to suit her. She looked back down at the map. She couldn't make sense of the cattle missing from a pattern of places along a path and a cut-through. But the pattern of it all wasn't a comfort. It was an annoying and painful hangnail. A puzzle she *should* be able to solve, but couldn't.

"Come to the game with me, Rosalie." He said it in that same straightforward, calm way he'd said "let me." An order, wrapped up in something that left room for her to say no.

Except deep down, she didn't want to, and she supposed he knew that, and it's why he said it that way.

Wanting aside, she *should* say no. She needed to keep

her eyes on the map—because if she looked at him, she'd forget all about *no*. She'd forget about too many things.

But she looked up at him, because it was hard to be a coward. That too-handsome face, that cocky smile. But there was something soft under all that. His connection to this place, his parents. His wanting to solve this murder to ease their worry . He would have grown up on that solid Kirk foundation, and as much as she wanted to believe that all his years away, all his fancy, high living could have—*would* have—changed him, she knew they hadn't.

He was a damn good man, and that was a damn big problem.

Problems had always been her weakness. "All right."

Chapter Eleven

Duncan had given Rosalie space after that. He had a bad feeling if he was around her too much, she'd change her mind.

So he'd taken her little biographical sketches on the different ranch hands back home. He'd gone over them, added his own notes to the margins. Tried to draw some conclusions and come up empty.

He'd gone up to his parents' for dinner, both to help them learn the new security system, and to get their take on Rosalie's sketches. But by the time he'd finally talked them into actually *using* the security system, and they'd sat down to dinner, he could only see how pale and *off* his father was and figured the sketches could wait.

He'd talk to Mom in the morning after Dad headed out for chores. She seemed sturdy enough to handle it, even if she was worried sick over Dad. So he'd made sure the security system was set, headed back to his cabin, then taken a pain pill and gone to bed. He'd actually slept well, and it had been a while on that front.

He supposed he'd taken Rosalie's advice from the other day and tried to take care of himself so he would be able to take care of his parents.

In the morning, he considered not wearing his sling. His

arm still ached, but wasn't it time to move on? He drank some coffee, choked down a protein bar, and took a pain pill while he considered it. In the end, he slid it on. He'd wear it today, leave it off tonight, and hope that there was some kind of progress there. And that he didn't have to remind himself and everyone else at a *baseball* game what had happened to him.

He drove up to the main house, which was empty as he walked through it. Empty and not locked up. He was going to be mad about that, but he spotted his mother from the window that looked out over the backyard. She was attacking her garden. And Duncan knew his mother and her moods well enough to know this was a stress-filled planting morning.

So he went out back to help. He approached as she ruthlessly hoed a line of dirt.

"What can I do?" he asked by way of greeting.

Mom wiped her forehead with the back of her forearm. Her gaze dipped to his arm in the sling. "I've got it handled, honey."

"You have to let me help, because I'm not going to be around tonight." He probably couldn't hoe much with his left hand, but he could plant. So he crouched next to the line of seedlings and started dropping them where he knew they belonged. He felt like a kid again, but in a kind of nostalgic, nice way.

"Where will you be tonight?" Mom asked, going back to the task of hoeing rows.

"I'm taking Rosalie to the Bent County High baseball game."

Mom sent him a doleful look. "That's not very romantic."

"First, I wasn't trying to be *romantic*. Second, baseball is very romantic, Mom."

"I went to every one of your high-school baseball games, Duncan. There is nothing romantic about a bunch of sweaty boys—and girls, Sarabeth *is* the talk of the county, aside from you being back—throwing a ball around."

It made him laugh in spite of himself. "Trust me. Rosalie wouldn't have agreed to dinner or much else. This is… we'll call it an easing-in."

"Mmm." Mom studied him. "Are you at least going to bring her flowers?"

"I'm going to bring her more information for our case," he replied, dropping the last plant for this row. It hurt a little, but he began to scoop the dirt over the roots.

Mom sighed heavily. "Duncan. Honestly."

"She won't trust flowers." Though it was tempting, just to see the narrow-eyed suspicion on her face. But since she was actually going out with him, he didn't want to rile her up too much. There was a fine, careful line with Rosalie that required some…finesse.

Luckily, he'd spent most of his adult life learning the fine art of when to finesse an off-speed pitch and when to blast one right down the middle.

When it came to Rosalie… "She doesn't trust much."

"No, I don't suppose she would." Mom's sigh was sympathetic this time. "I could throttle Tim Young for what he did to those girls. If he was alive. Joan too, for that matter. But make sure you understand, just because Audra got all the sweet, and Rosalie got all the sour, doesn't mean she's not tender under all that bite."

He glanced up at his mother. Her cheeks were a little red from how hard she'd been working, and she scowled down at him like he'd done something wrong.

"You warning me off all of a sudden?"

"No, I'm not warning you *off*." She puffed out a breath. "Haven't I been the one…? Oh, never mind. My point is… That girl is so busy looking out for everyone else, including us, by looking into this murder, even though she doesn't have to. I just want you to understand, you should be looking out for her."

It amused him that's how his mother looked at it, that it would annoy Rosalie to be *looked after*, that it was exactly what he wanted to do anyway. He'd spent most of the past fifteen years—longer maybe—not being selfish, necessarily. The last few years he'd mentored some rookies, he'd given back, but that had always been about baseball. And sometimes that bled over into the personal if a teammate was making some bad choices off the field, but he'd never had the time, *taken* the time, to take care of anyone who mattered to him just because of who they were.

His parents. A friend—romantic or not—that didn't connect to a baseball uniform.

Even though he wished it wasn't *murder*, he was glad to be here, taking care where he could. Whether Mom, Dad, or Rosalie liked it or not.

"I do understand that," Duncan said, getting back to his feet and brushing off his dirty knees with his good hand. "And you know why I do?"

"Because she's got a pretty face?"

"Because my mama raised me right." Being back home gave him a new perspective on how everything he'd managed to build as a professional athlete had been built on the foundation his parents, and this ranch, had laid.

She made a scoffing noise, but her mouth curved. "I should hope so. We'll see how long that sweet talk lasts when I task you with my next favor. I don't suppose you can think of a way to follow your father around this morning without making him think we're trying to babysit him? I'd rather you do that than ruin my garden by continuing to plant my cowpeas too close together."

"I'll see what I can·do," he said, ignoring her old complaint. She used to joke she'd put him in T-ball just so she could plant her garden right.

Then both his parents had sacrificed a whole hell of a lot, all because he'd fallen in love with a game. And he wanted to pay them back the only way he thought they might accept. By figuring this damn murder out.

"But first, I want you to tell me more about Owen."

Mom blew out a breath and squinted out toward the bunkhouse. "I didn't have much interaction with the boy before the murder. I remember the first week he was here, Terry had some complaints about the both of them. Lazy work. Bad attitudes. Dad, of course, asked Terry to be patient."

"Was he?"

"Always," Mom said loyally. "Kept complaining for quite some time, but no threats to turn them out. It takes time to work the lazy out of boys who've never been given a chance."

"And when do you think they worked it out of them?"

"Your father would have a better grasp on timing." Her eyebrows drew together, as if she was trying to think back. "I can't remember when the tide really turned. Sometime after Christmas I'd have to guess."

"So they've been model hands these past few months?"

"Model? No. Efficient? Not really. Better? Yes. Improvement. I had high hopes for Hunter. Less for Owen, but that's probably how I feel about your father's family coloring my perspective." She glanced toward the bunkhouse again. "Poor boy has been nothing but grief-stricken since. I asked him if he wanted to go home, be with family, and he begged me to stay. Said he'd worked twice as hard, enough for him and Hunter. Just begged me not to send him away."

"Something back home scares him?"

"I don't know about that. I just don't think anyone cares about him back there, poor kid. And not that Terry *cares*, but he takes good care of those boys. So does your father. This is a good place to be."

That sentiment stayed with Duncan as he went about his day. Helped with a few ranch chores he could do one-handed, talked with some of the hands, shared a sandwich with Terry at lunchtime. He tried to poke into Owen, and Hunter for that matter, without being too obvious about it.

Not one of them, Dad included, would give the two compliments on their work ethic, but the consensus among the hands matched up with Mom's. They'd been improving.

This is a good place to be.

Except someone had been murdered. Right there, in his own front yard, and the cops hadn't found any answers yet.

So if they wouldn't, he and Rosalie would have to.

IT WASN'T A DATE. Rosalie told herself that as she debated for far too long about what to wear. It was a high-school baseball game. So jeans and a T-shirt and she needed to stop overthinking *which* T-shirt.

But she considered about ten different options, told herself to wear her ratty old Bent County High School T-shirt, and ended up pulling on the form-fitting V-neck the color of her eyes. She considered her hair next. She should just throw it up and slap a hat on it, but she didn't. She took time—too much time—curling the careful strands she pulled out of the ponytail. Then putting on makeup—

ridiculous, just ridiculous—with a deft hand to make sure it didn't look like she was wearing any.

When she was done with that, irritated with herself, irritable with the situation, so damn nervous she thought she'd be sick, she marched herself downstairs.

"It's just a baseball game," she muttered to herself. But just as she got downstairs, the front door opened and Audra stepped in.

Rosalie had been hoping to escape before Audra was done for the day. But there was no way around her sister, standing there in front of the door. "Hey," she offered.

"Headed out?" Audra asked, innocently enough, nodding toward the purse Rosalie carried.

"Yeah." Rosalie let the silence stretch out. Maybe Audra would hear it through the grapevine, maybe Rosalie would feel like talking about it *after*, but she was not about to let Audra think she was going out on a date with Duncan.

Because she wasn't.

"You've been avoiding me," Audra said.

There was no point in denying it, and it was better than talking about Duncan. "Yep."

"You can't forever."

"You'd be surprised."

"Rosalie."

"I can't talk about our parents tonight, sis," she said brightly. "I'm going to the baseball game. You know…" It dawned on her, quick and perfect. "You and Franny should come."

Audra's eyes narrowed. "On your date with Duncan?"

"It's not a date," she immediately snapped. Then stopped short. "How did you know I was going with Duncan?"

For a moment, Audra stood there with a kind of surprised look on her face that Rosalie couldn't figure out.

Then Audra shook her head, but her cheeks were turning red. "Natalie mentioned it in passing," she said with a shrug.

"Why are you acting guilty?"

Audra made a dismissive noise, then cocked her head. "Is that him?" She opened the door behind her, and there was Duncan's truck bumping up the gravel lane.

Nerves seemed to full-on explode in Rosalie's chest, and she didn't know what the hell to do with that feeling. The only time she ever got nervous was when something at work went south, but even that she usually brazened her way through.

All of her brazenness wasn't enough to get through Duncan Kirk. But she could do it, would do it, if she had company. Support. *Distraction.*

"Look, just because Duncan's driving doesn't mean you and Franny can't come. It's not a date. It's just…a get-together. To support Sarabeth and our alma mater."

"Franny didn't go to Bent County, and I've got things to do. You're going out, have fun." Audra grabbed her by the arm and pulled her to the door. "And if you end up not coming home tonight, you just make sure to text me so I don't worry."

Rosalie had never been embarrassed about sex. In fact, she liked to flaunt it in Audra's face, because Audra was usually the one being a little prudish about it. But this was…different. Why was everything about Duncan different? "I am coming home tonight, Audra," she said firmly. Because it was *just* a baseball game.

"Then you don't have to text me. And we can have a nice long talk about our parents when you get back."

She blinked at her sister. "Are you trying to blackmail me into having sex with Duncan?"

"If it helps." Audra gave her a shove out the door as

Duncan pulled to a stop. He got out of his truck, offered a wave with his good arm.

"Hi, Duncan," Audra called with a return wave. "You two have fun. I won't wait up." Then she closed the front door behind her, and locked the door, as if Rosalie didn't have her own key.

But there was no going back now, because Duncan was here. Looking like he always did. Casual jeans, work boots that looked a little on the new side, a plain navy blue T-shirt, and a baseball cap, also plain. No doubt because he didn't want to draw attention to the fact he was Duncan Kirk, former professional baseball player. She also noted he wasn't wearing his sling.

"You got a doctor's note?" she demanded, pointing at his arm, trying to determine if he was holding it more awkwardly than the other one.

"You going to tell on me?"

"Maybe."

"Uncool." But he grinned at her. "I'm allowed to take it off for a few hours a day. I'm taking my few hours. You ready to go?"

She nodded, hoping it didn't come off as jerky as it felt. She moved in his direction, reminding herself it wasn't a damn date. She climbed up into his truck. It still smelled like new, and that did nothing to ease these knots inside of her. Because it all felt new, when it damn well shouldn't.

"I can drive if it's bad on your arm."

"I got it," he replied easily, and he did seem to have it. He turned around and drove down the lane, then toward the highway without any winces that she could see as she studied his face, waiting for one.

"I brought your list of ranch hands with some added information," he said, eyes on the road. "In the back seat, if you're interested."

She reached back and picked up the pieces of paper. She skimmed through the sloppily written additions. "Am I supposed to be able to read this chicken scratch?"

"Sorry. Bad arm. I can read it to you. Some of it is stuff I knew, some of it is stuff I got out of people today. But I just keep coming back to Owen and Hunter. The detectives haven't come up with anything that ties Hunter's former life to here, but there's got to be something there, doesn't there? They were in trouble in North Dakota. There was no trouble here. Then all the sudden, he's dead. And Owen's not."

"You suspect Owen?" Rosalie asked, surprised. She hadn't thought he would.

"I don't know. It just seems too much of a coincidence. I talked to Mom and Dad today, about Owen and Hunter. How they were lazy whiners when they first arrived, but slowly over time got a little less whiny. But still lazy."

"Makes sense."

"I guess. But Dad told me when he thought they kind of started to turn things around in the helpful department. And it seems weird as hell to me that their slight changes of heart coincide with the first cow's death."

Rosalie turned that over with everything she knew. Did it connect? They had to look into everything, she supposed. She thought about Owen that day when he'd yelled for help. And after, when she'd questioned him. "He was genuinely grieving." Though that didn't mean anything, but she wanted to hear how Duncan would argue his theory.

"I think so too. But people can grieve things, even when they have something to do with the end result."

Wasn't that the truth? "Did Owen have a way of getting into your parents' house?"

Duncan's gaze slid to hers. "I'm not sure, but I'd bet he would. You heard from the cops about those guns?"

She shook her head. "No. Tests will take a few days, I imagine. They probably had to send them away. They're still working on expanding their crime-scene-investigation unit, so not everything can be done in house, and then you gotta wait."

"It doesn't make sense to me that Owen would go through all that trouble, then have us find the body. Seems a stretch. But there's just something about those two that doesn't add up."

Rosalie couldn't help but agree. She read through Duncan's sloppy notes again. "We'll keep digging," she said, as much to him as herself.

The truck came to a stop and Rosalie looked up. They were in the high-school parking lot.

Duncan shifted the truck into Park, then turned to face her. "All right. No more shop talk. Just baseball and hot dogs, Red."

It was easy, she told herself. Just two people at a baseball game. So she hopped out of the truck and walked with him toward the field. A decent crowd for a high-school baseball game. He bought the hot dogs from a bored-looking teen at the concession stand and they walked toward the bleachers to find a seat among the crowd.

"That's the Sarabeth cheering section," she said, pointing to about half of the bleachers. She waved at Quinn as she led Duncan forward. "There are six Thompson brothers, and one of them married Sarabeth's mom. The rest are all married and half of them are procreating. Makes for quite a racket. Hope you're ready."

"I played in Dodger Stadium, Rosalie."

"Such a big shot." She was going to rib him some more,

but she spotted Sarabeth waving wildly. She pointed over to the dugout. "Your biggest fan has spotted you."

Duncan turned, gave Sarabeth a wave. She beamed at him, clutching her glove to her chest.

"There's no accounting for taste," Rosalie muttered, but she was smiling in spite of herself, because… Oh, she was a big, dumb softy.

They found a place in the bleachers, and Duncan maneuvered himself in first. "Here. Sit on my right side."

"Why?"

"So I can do this." He casually rested his arm across her shoulders.

She should push it off.

But she didn't. She settled in and watched Sarabeth pitch while the crowd went wild around them, and Duncan watched with avid interest. So much interest, she found herself watching *him* a little too much. The way she could see the wheels in his head turning with every play, the way he got into it, whistling and cheering on Sarabeth just like her family was.

She felt it, deep inside, the slow, horrible unlocking of her heart. She would have tightened it up, added fifty more locks, thrown away every last key, if she thought it'd do any good.

But sitting next to him like this, watching him enjoy himself, it just felt inevitable.

Inevitable doom.

Chapter Twelve

Duncan had forgotten how much he loved baseball. As a spectator. It wasn't just that he'd been good as a kid—he'd loved the game. The intricacies of it. The teamwork required. That feeling of being in a crowd holding their breath while everyone waited for the next pitch.

It's a good place to be. His mother's words kept echoing in his head. Because it *was*. Bent County wasn't perfect. Hell, even the Kirk Ranch wasn't perfect. But there was a community, a teamwork to it. Just like baseball.

Maybe Owen Green had come from a not-so-nice place. Maybe that explained why his demeanor had changed slowly, as had Hunter's, over their first months of being here.

He hated that even in the middle of the fun, and a date with Rosalie, his mind kept trailing back to Owen and Hunter. A dead body. A distraught young man.

Two outsiders.

When the game was over, a close and tense win for Bent County High, what Duncan really wanted to do was disappear, but he couldn't quite bring himself to do it.

Maybe he didn't really know Sarabeth from any other kid around here. They weren't kin, and as far as he knew his parents weren't acquainted with the Thompsons. But he couldn't forget who he'd been out there on the field, and if a major league player had come to one of his games?

Hell.

"Go on, Ace. Give 'em a thrill," Rosalie said, giving him a nudge toward the dugout, where the coaches were talking to the kids, but all eyes were on him.

The excitement was palpable as he approached—from both kids and coaches alike. It was a different staff than when he'd played here, so he didn't recognize any of the coaches. He introduced himself to the head coach, and then he was essentially engulfed.

He gave compliments. Signed balls, gloves, and bats. Answered a zillion questions. Politely declined a job assistant-coaching…three times. Then, in an attempt to escape, had to shake what felt like a million parent hands until his arm was throbbing.

Eventually the crowds began to dissipate a *little*, but Duncan had officially had enough. He searched the area for Rosalie, found her underneath a tree, watching him with amusement.

Save me, he mouthed at her.

She grinned at him but pushed off the tree and sauntered over. Smooth as could be, she extracted him from a small group of overzealous adults without making either of them look like jerks.

"You're a real pro," he said. "I'd have hired you back in LA."

She shook her head at that. "You're too nice to those people."

"Can't really have it getting around town that LA changed me and I'm some snooty SOB now. My mother would have my neck."

It got a good laugh out of her, and since they were back

at his truck, in the shadow of it and a tree, and most of the parking lot had cleared out, he went ahead and followed the path of that laugh.

Because his life had been ruled by discipline for so long, there was something freeing and irresistible about following an impulse, a temptation.

So he pressed his mouth to hers, caging her subtly against his truck, the size of his frame no doubt obscuring her from any straggling crowd members.

He half expected her to push him away, but she didn't. She melted into him like wax. When he wrapped his good arm around her back and pulled her tight against him, she raised her hands to clasp around the back of his neck.

Maybe it was the location, maybe it was Rosalie, but there was a kind of sweet nostalgia to it all. But underneath that sweetness, and the smell of baseball, and a crisp Wyoming night, was the sharpening edge of need.

The throb in his shoulder twinged with the drugging pulse of pleasure. A strange, potent mix of feelings wrapped up in the faint strawberry scent of her.

She didn't push him away, but she did ease back. He could only barely make out her face in the dark. "We're in a parking lot, Ace."

But her breath came out on a little sigh, and her hand was still curled around his neck.

"Yeah, we are. Did you ever make out in this parking lot after hours back in your day?"

She looked around—the baseball diamond was dark now. The school behind them was dark. "A lady never tells." Then her eyes narrowed. "What about you?"

He put a hand to his chest in mock outrage. "A gentleman never tells either."

She snorted.

And because she did, and because she hadn't taken her arms down from around him, he lowered his mouth again. This time with a little more of that urgency he was starting to feel, and a nip against her bottom lip.

"Come home with me," he murmured against her mouth. Not charming, he knew, but she pulled something out of him. A directness. A straightforward need. Like a bright new light, after quite a few months of existing and maybe even wallowing in the dark.

He could feel the inner battle going on inside of her. But he was getting the picture that her internal battles weren't about him specifically. They were about stuff going on in her life.

Still, when the battle ended, and she said, "Maybe for a minute or two," he considered it a win.

It didn't mean she was going to sleep with him.

Rosalie told herself this, over and over again, as his truck drove down the highway and a mournful country song twanged around them in the dark of the truck's interior.

But if she *did* sleep with him, then it might eradicate this…*this*.

Like something had wrapped around her lungs, tight and with thorns. A bramble bush inside of her chest.

It went away when he kissed her. Everything did, except the delicious lick of heat. Her lungs could expand when he kissed her. She didn't *worry* when his arm banded around her. All those doubts and concerns just evaporated.

So it could just be sex. She could handle just sex. A little fling with the hot neighbor guy. She was good at flings and handling men. She was a *pro*.

Even as he pulled onto the service-road entrance to his family ranch, rather than the main entrance that would lead to his parents' house. Even as he pulled up to his cabin at the back of the property. Even as he turned off the car and hopped out, she told herself it was just a bit of fun.

And once they got a little bit of fun out of their systems, they could just…move on. No harm, no foul.

She slid out of the truck as he did, still not saying anything. She met him at the front of the truck in the little porchlight that barely illuminated the little patch of yard they were in. He was so tall, so handsome, there in the moonlight.

So much potential harm, she knew, as her heart lurched, and beat unsteadily in her chest as they stood there just staring at each other. She managed to swallow, to look away, up at the stars to steady herself.

It was a riot of stars, universes up there, bright and vast. She had only ever lived here, looking up at *this* sky, without light pollution, without an entire world out there that Duncan had gone out and experienced.

"Miss this out in LA?" she asked, and maybe she meant it as a little dig aimed at his time away, but really, she was curious. What had he missed about home while out in California living his dream?

"Yeah. Yeah, I did. I used to lay out under the stars after every game here—win or lose—and picture myself under the lights of a professional ballpark. People chanting my name."

"And you got it."

"I got it, and then there was nowhere to lay outside and watch the stars. I mean there was, but it wasn't home. I never regretted it. I don't, even now, even when it didn't end in a nice little bow like I wanted it to. But that doesn't mean I didn't miss this as much as I enjoyed that."

It was somehow the perfect answer. A blend of understanding how lucky he was, without losing sight of where he'd come from. Why did that lodge in her chest like physical pain?

At least until he moved closer, drew her into his arms, and kissed her. Soft and sweet at first. A kiss meant for starlight and the chill of a Wyoming night she didn't feel because his body gave out warmth and stirred up some inside her as well.

But the angle changed, the grip. Everything got a little deeper, hotter, needier, and that was exactly what she needed. Ride the wave, forget about all the messy emotions cluttering up inside of her. She'd deal with those later, alone. Pick them apart, set them away.

They moved toward the cabin, arms wrapped around each other, mouths on each other. A laugh when they tripped, a shuddery exhale when his hand slid under her shirt, spread out on her back. Hot, big, rough.

They somehow managed to stumble up the stairs to his door, and he opened it without even taking his mouth from hers. She would have told him it was impressive, but he nibbled at her bottom lip, taking away all rational thought. He pulled her in, backing them into his living room.

She heard something *crunch* under her shoe. Confused, she blinked her eyes open even as Duncan's mouth took a very interesting tour of her neck.

But the sensual haze faded into cold fear as she saw the room around them. "Oh my God."

"If you think that's impressive…"

She choked on a half laugh, even in the midst of the mess. "No, Duncan." She pushed at his chest. "God. Your place is trashed."

He turned then and saw what she saw. His face went utterly blank.

All his boxes had been upended. Trophies—some broken, some shattered. Clothes strewn about, drawers opened and emptied.

"What the hell?"

"We need to call the police, Duncan," she said sharply. She felt a bubble of panic try to burst free, but she pushed it back down. Because this wasn't murder. They didn't know what it was, but things could be replaced, so it wasn't *murder*.

But because there *had* been a murder, it was more terrifying than just a break-in.

When Duncan didn't move, Rosalie pulled out her own phone, irritated that her hand shook. She hesitated for a moment, not sure what decision to make, then went ahead and dialed Copeland's cell.

Maybe this didn't relate to the murder, but how could it not?

"Do I even want to know why you're calling my personal number and not Bent County?" he answered, as she tried to push away from Duncan.

Who held on to her. Tightly.

"There was a break-in at Duncan's cabin," Rosalie said without sounding panicked. She hoped. "Someone broke in and trashed his place."

He grunted. "Call the emergency line then."

"Copeland."

The long, world-weary sigh on the other end was dramatic. "Yeah, yeah, I'm coming. I'll handle it."

The line went dead, and Rosalie put the phone back in her pocket. She surveyed the room again. "Duncan…" She felt helpless and strange, and that wasn't *her*, so she dug deep for some kind of control. "We should wait outside," she decided. No contaminating a crime scene. "We should… Duncan, you're going to have to tell your parents. When the police come up the drive, they'll see."

"Call the detective back. Have him cut through. I'll…" Then he cursed and took off, back out the door and into the dark night. She realized, only a second or two after he did, what he might be worried about. So she took off after him.

She ran after him—he was a quick shadow in the dark— across fields. She even had to hop a fence and wondered how he'd done it with his bad arm. The main house was fully dark in the distance. His long legs, and maybe the whole being-a-professional-athlete thing, meant he made it to the front of the house before her. He was peering into the window on the front door when she caught up, lungs burning and eyes watering.

"Everything looks fine from here. The security system is set." He was breathing heavily. She could tell he was in pain, but he didn't reach up and grip his shoulder.

She hated to say it, but she knew she had to. "You're still going to have to wake them up," she said around panting breaths. "You don't want them to wake up to cops coming up the drive. They'll think something worse happened."

He inhaled deeply, let it out slowly, evening his breathing quicker than she was able to. "Yeah. Why don't you call Audra. Have her pick you up?"

She was surprised that the words landed like little stabs of pain. That damn bramble being yanked out of her heart. But she managed to keep her tone even, light. "Is that what you want?"

He stared at her there in the dim glow of the ranch's security light. "No," he said, and with enough heft and weight that those little brambles dug right back into her heart.

She swallowed it all down. "Then I'll stay."

Chapter Thirteen

"Let's go over this one more time. You don't know if the door was locked or not?"

Duncan sighed. He was in all kinds of pain, but the cops wouldn't let him into his cabin to grab a pill. Rosalie had somehow, after quite a while, convinced his parents to go back up to the house and try to get some sleep, so there was *that*.

He knew they wouldn't sleep, but at least they wouldn't stand out in the increasing cold and worry. They could worry comfortably and inside.

"I've told each and every one of you," Duncan said, trying not to be irritable. "I locked the door before I left. When I got back, I was distracted." He'd settled on that word about the third time they'd asked this same damn question. "I unlocked the door, but it's not like I tested the knob. I just jabbed my key in and twisted, and assumed that's what unlocked the door. Until I stepped inside to all that."

There were cops crawling around his cabin, all the lights on and blazing. He wanted to be grateful they were taking this seriously, but he was in some serious pain, and worried about his parents and what this *meant*.

Detective Beckett approached him and the uniformed deputy that had been asking the *same damn questions*.

"We've taken pictures. The guys are working on trying to lift some prints right now. You'll need to go through and see what's missing, but as much as some of that stuff might be a gold mine, most of it is personalized and unique enough, selling would come back on the seller. They were no doubt looking for easy items. Cash. Guns."

"I don't keep a gun down here." His shoulder ached. A migraine had started drumming at his temples. Rosalie's hand rubbed up and down his back, but he barely felt it. "If I had cash, it was nothing major."

"Can't one of the deputies bring him out one of his pain pills? Some water?" Rosalie demanded.

"Why are you here again?" Copeland asked her.

"To ruin your life," she replied, and almost, *almost* made Duncan smile. "He's in pain, Copeland."

The detective huffed out a breath. "Where do you keep them?"

"Cabinet above the stove."

Detective Beckett grunted, then stalked back to the cabin. Rosalie didn't stop rubbing Duncan's back.

"Getting prints is good. We saw the mess they left. They'd have touched something, and there's no way they had the sense to wipe it all down with a mess like that."

She was surprisingly comforting when she wanted to be. "And then what?"

"And then we see if it connects to the murder. If it does, this might be a real big break."

God, he hoped so.

Detective Beckett came back a few minutes later, but there was nothing in his hands. His expression was grimmer than it had been.

"Well, I think we figured out what they were after, or

at least what they took. Bottle's empty. No chance it was empty, and you just forgot?"

Empty… Duncan shook his head. "No. No possible way."

"How many do you think you had left?"

Duncan blew out a breath. "Most of the bottle. I only take them sporadically. I'm not sure I could give an exact count, but I could get close if I sit down and think about it."

"You do that. Once we clear you to go in, you make a list of anything that's missing in as much annoying detail as you can manage." He glanced at Rosalie with a little sneer. "Have her help. She knows what we're looking for."

She smirked at Copeland. "Flatterer."

He rolled his eyes and strode away, back into the cabin, which was swarming with deputies. Well, it wasn't *really* a swarm, it just felt like that.

"How about some ibuprofen or something. Will that take the edge off?"

"If I take a whole bottle," he muttered irritably. "Listen. Hell, it's late, and I'm not fit to be around anyone. You should head on home. I'll drive you—"

"Are you going to go up to your parents and sleep there if you drive me home?"

He surveyed the strange landscape in front of him. His cabin. His things. Cops everywhere. "No, I won't be able to sleep until I go through everything. See what they took besides my damn pills."

"Then I'm staying with. Detective's orders, remember?"

"You don't have to, Rosalie."

"Who said anything about having to? I'll have you know, I don't do anything I *have* to. Except pay taxes maybe."

It surprised a little laugh out of him, unbanded the tiniest bit of tension in his chest. He pulled her to him, rested his chin on the top of her head. "Thanks, Red." For a minute, he was almost able to relax a little bit.

But then the detective came out of the cabin and walked over to them. "You can go in and clean up."

Duncan watched as Copeland seemed to take notice of his arm around Rosalie.

"Get me that list as soon as you're able." Then he stalked away. Not angry, exactly. Just purposeful. The deputies were leaving the cabin too. Getting in cars, talking to each other as they did.

Duncan found that all of a sudden he didn't want to go inside. Didn't want to see or even begin to think about cleaning up or sorting through what he might still have, and what he might not.

So he focused on the little niggling thing that settled in his brain whenever Rosalie and Copeland were around each other.

"You ever have a thing with the detective?"

Rosalie looked up at him, and even in the dim light, he could see confusion on her face. Followed by amusement. "Define *a thing*?"

He scowled at her. "The point is the lack of definition. *Thing* could be anything. That's my point."

"Does it matter?" she asked, her expression sober, even as amusement danced in her eyes. She *liked* making him uncomfortable, and that should be some kind of turnoff. But it wasn't.

"It doesn't *matter*," he replied, calmly if he did say so himself. "I'm just curious."

"Curious or jealous?"

He looked down at her, matched her smug expression with one of his own. "Does *that* matter?"

She held his gaze for a minute, then shook her head on

a sigh. "I don't mind jealous. I don't mind curious. Never looked in that direction. Actually kind of hated him until a few months ago."

"What happened a few months ago?"

"He worked on a case involving my cousin, Vi. Hart's wife. She was kidnapped by her abusive ex." Rosalie shuddered, and he found it was his turn to rub a comforting hand up and down her back. "Anyway, Copeland worked his ass off to help us find Vi. Hard to keep hating the guy after that. Though he tries to make it easy."

Duncan chuckled. But it died, because...

"We can keep avoiding it, Ace, but it's still going to be there."

"Yeah," he agreed, stepping toward the cabin with her. Avoiding it wasn't going to change anything. And at the very least, he had a *we*.

Rosalie was dragging, and she knew Duncan was too. She'd tried to clean up as they went along, particularly the shattered glass, and he tried to remember what he had packed away in boxes that might be missing.

She'd coaxed him into taking some ibuprofen as they worked, but even after hours had passed, he hadn't come up with anything to add to the list of missing items to go along with his pain pills.

When he'd stood in the same place for a good two minutes, just staring at some fancy engraved plate in his hand, she crossed to him, took it out of his grasp, and placed it in a box. "Come on, Ace, you're beat. Let's take a break, get some rest."

"I'm pissed," he corrected. He flung his good arm toward the front of the cabin. "It would have taken someone who knew their way around to get back here without passing by the main house."

"Maybe," Rosalie said, considering the layout of the Kirk Ranch. "Or they could have turned off their headlights. Used Neutral to cruise down the drive to your place. They could have known about the cut-throughs because they've been ranching these parts for years. There's a lot of explanations."

"They would have to know this cabin was back here, and that there might be something valuable in it. Because *I'm* in it. It wasn't random, or they'd burglarize Mom and Dad's, which makes me sick to think about."

She rubbed a hand up and down his arm. "It wouldn't take much for someone to know all that, Duncan. I bet all of Bent County knows more of your business than you'd ever be comfortable with."

He scowled at that. "Down to my pain pills?"

"Afraid so." She could tell that *really* didn't sit well with him, but it was true. Maybe Bent County was a big place geographically, but interesting tidbits spread through all the small towns like wildfire.

He sank onto the couch. "Maybe other things are gone, but if they are, they're small, inconsequential things I don't remember. All my awards are here. I couldn't tell you if they slipped out with a jersey, or ball or bat, or whatever the hell. There's just nothing of any value that's gone, I don't think."

She settled next to him on the couch. "Well, like Copeland said, the awards are too specific. No resale value. What about watches or… I don't know, what do rich guys buy?" She was hoping to get a little bit of a smile out of him, but his scowl didn't budge.

"Cars. Nice houses. All of which I got rid of when I

moved home. I didn't even bother to keep expensive suits or shoes. Why would I?"

"Okay, fair enough, but someone who knows you're a professional baseball player wouldn't necessarily know that. Maybe they came looking for cash, couldn't find it, and bailed."

"Just stumbled upon the pills?"

"Maybe."

He looked over at her then. Shadows in his eyes, mouth downturned showing off grooves bracketing his lips. Beat clean up. She wanted to reach out and smooth the tuft of hair that was sticking up where he'd raked his fingers through it, but it felt like an intimacy that bordered too close to a bunch of things she just wasn't sure about yet.

"You don't sound convinced," he said, and because he sounded so damn distraught, she didn't resist the urge. She reached out, smoothed her hand over his hair. And it felt good. To reach out and soothe.

"I would be convinced. If not for the murder," she said gently. She kept her arm around him. "Coincidences happen all the time, but this feels like a stretch to think they aren't connected considering your parents haven't had criminal issues at the ranch before, except the missing cows. Which I still think might be connected." A lot of connections, but no answers. Still, that was an investigation. Steps, connections, and little threads, until you found the thing that bound them all together.

Connections, but not obvious ones. She looked around the trashed room. Silly just to do for some pain pills, but... "Maybe whoever did this was looking for something specific if they didn't take anything."

"They took the pills."

"Yes, but surely someone capable of murder is capable of

scoring their own drugs without creating this mess. What about weapons?"

"Like I told the cops, I don't have guns down here."

"Maybe they didn't know that. Maybe they were looking for something else."

"I thought everyone knew everything."

She sighed, feeling nothing but sympathy for him. "You're getting grumpy."

"No shit."

"Get some rest, huh? I'll call Copeland and tell him you know how many pills you think were stolen and that's all we found. If you think of anything else, we'll let him know, but you need some rest."

She started to get up, but he grabbed her arm. So she stood by the couch but couldn't step away because he held her hand firmly.

"You've been up as long as I have."

"Yeah, but I haven't had my shoulder recently reattached, so I'm just a little tired, not exhausted and in pain."

"I took some damn ibuprofen."

"Yeah, it really helped. Come on, you big baby, I'll tuck you in."

He raised an eyebrow, and she laughed in spite of herself.

"Mind out of the gutter." She pulled him up, making sure it was his good arm before she yanked. He got to his feet.

"My mind doesn't have much juice left to find itself in the gutter, but I could work on it."

She pushed him gently to the bedroom. "I'm sure you could, but not tonight. Or this morning, or whatever it is." She nudged him into a sitting position on his unmade bed. There hadn't been any broken glass in here, just upended drawers and a trashed closet. "Take off your shoes," she told him.

He grunted, then toed off the shoes.

"Lay down," she ordered, waiting for him to balk at being told what to do. But he really *was* tired, because he did as he was told. And he held out his good arm.

"Lay down with me, Rosalie," he said, in the same kind of authoritative tone she'd used on him.

She didn't like the idea of him sleeping alone in this place that didn't have a security system. That had been violated in some way. Maybe it wouldn't make sense for a burglar to come back, but none of this made much sense.

So she moved over to the opposite side of the bed. She didn't pull any covers over her, but she lied down on her back, staring up at the ceiling.

But Duncan reached over, snuck his good arm under her, and pulled her close to him. She might have balked at it, but she could *feel* him relax. The tension leaked out of him as he exhaled.

Which somehow made her worry worse. Because this felt too good and there was nothing good about what was going on. "Once you've gotten some rest, we're calling Cam Delaney and getting a security system for this place."

"Are we?"

She could feel him falling asleep almost immediately, so she didn't say anything else. Just lied there.

While she stayed awake, protecting them both.

Chapter Fourteen

Duncan woke up with a curse on his lips as a sharp zing of pain shot from his shoulder down his arm. Grumbling irritably, he blinked his eyes open. Everything about last night came rushing back at him and made him want to close his eyes and go back to sleep.

But Rosalie wasn't here and he wanted to know where she went, so he forced himself to sit up. He scrubbed a hand over his face while his opposite shoulder throbbed. Just throbbed.

It was to be expected. It wasn't a career-ending injury and two surgeries for nothing. But he was damn tired of it, and he didn't have a real pain pill to take the edge off. Because someone had trashed his stuff and stolen his pills.

Rosalie was right that it had to connect, but that it didn't make much sense in the grand scheme of things. Missing cows. Murder. Missing pills.

He scrubbed a hand over his face again. Coffee. He smelled it, and he needed some. Then he and Rosalie could sit down and plan out what to do next.

But when he moved into the kitchen, it wasn't Rosalie in his house. It was Mom. She was wiping down his kitchen counter and Rosalie was nowhere to be seen.

She looked up at him, surveyed him in that way she

had when he'd been sick as a kid and insisted he was well enough to go to baseball practice anyway.

"She had to go into her office," Mom said, even though he hadn't asked about Rosalie. "I'm not sure she slept, poor girl. But she's as stubborn as you are."

"More."

Mom shook her head with a tiny smile. "Impossible."

"What about you? Any rest?"

"I tried. Slept in snatches, I suppose." She rinsed out the dishcloth, folded it neatly over the faucet.

"How's Dad holding up?"

Mom didn't look at him and didn't speak right away. That's how Duncan knew it was bad.

"He was out before dawn. Calving season is in full swing and we're down a hand. He's got lots of work to throw himself into. For good or for ill."

"I wish I could be more help."

"Next year you will be."

Duncan smiled. It was a nice enough thought. To know he'd be here next year and the year after. That he'd be in better physical shape to really help Dad out. But he sure as hell hoped they weren't dealing with any of this next year.

Still, he didn't say that to Mom. He just nodded in agreement and took the mug of coffee she offered him.

"Rosalie left you a list of things to do."

"Did she?"

Mom held out the paper, and in an only kind of legible chicken scratch there was a bulleted list.

- *Call your doctor get prescription refilled.*
- *Call Cam Delaney. Security system installed TODAY.*
- *Eat something and take care of yourself.*

Nothing about the case. Which no doubt meant she'd gone into her office so she could work on it alone.

Wasn't going to happen.

He was tempted to crumple the list, but she wasn't wrong about the first two things. Getting a security system up and running for his cabin would be necessary if he was going to have more pills on hand and wanted to feel safe about it.

But he hated the idea of Rosalie down at her office, investigating this case that involved everything he held dear without him.

"I've got a favor to ask you, Mom."

"Anything, honey."

"I've got a few calls to make. If I get an appointment set up for the alarm install, can you be here for it?"

"Where are you going to be?"

"I'll probably have to go into Fairmont to pick up my pills."

"And you can't plan that around a security install?"

He supposed there was no point trying to hedge with Mom. Even if she didn't figure it out, someone would see his truck in Wilde and no doubt tell her. "Okay, fine, I'm going to stop by Fool's Gold and talk to Rosalie." He looked down at the list with a scowl. "She's not shaking me off of this."

"Investigating is her job, her expertise. Is she shaking you off or is she just doing her job?"

Duncan didn't know quite how to respond to that. Mom wasn't wrong, but this was… It was a unique circumstance. Her job involved *him*. This ranch. His family. "You want me to just sit around and stew?"

"I want you to be safe."

Guilt was a sharp pang in his heart, but he didn't let it take over what had to be done. "I'm not in any danger. This all happened while I wasn't here. The murder happened when no one was around. Whatever's going on doesn't connect to us. You don't have to worry about me being safe. We're all safe."

"Duncan."

He hated the way his mother sounded. So…beaten down. Distraught. That just wasn't her. She had endless patience and optimism that everything could work out with enough hard work.

She sighed. "I want to believe some stranger came in and did both these things. I know that's what your father believes. And I'm trying so hard, but…"

He knew what she was going to say, and he hated it, but he felt that way too. "But it feels like an inside job."

Mom nodded. There were tears in her eyes, but they didn't fall. "It's one of our own. I just know it."

ROSALIE KNEW THE reception from the detectives wouldn't be positive, but maybe that's why she went. She wanted an argument. She was itching for a fight. Why not have it with Copeland?

Not smart when she was riding on the fumes of sleep deprivation, but she didn't want to be smart or patient, or depend on any of her usual investigative techniques. *Usually* the job itself kept her in line.

Except when the client mattered personally to her. Then her lines got a little blurry.

She wanted action and answers, and for this damn thing to be over. Because all she could seem to think about, worry about, *obsess* over, was how bereft Mr. and Mrs. Kirk had looked. How beaten down and exhausted Duncan was.

Even in sleep, when she'd slid out of bed maybe having dozed for less than an hour herself, he'd looked beat up, lying there, breathing evenly. Handsome as a devil but beat *up*.

Police investigations were full of waiting. Full of time ticking. Funny how easy that was to understand when she didn't really know the victim, and how impossible and unfair it felt when the crime was mixed up with people she knew and cared about.

And because she did *care* about Duncan in uncomfortable ways, she was going to throw her whole self into getting answers *fast*. Better than dealing with all that care.

She strode into the sheriff's department with a grim smile on her face. She made a beeline for the detective's office and was gratified to find all three of the detectives in there. Clearly having a little meeting.

Before she could even open her mouth for an obnoxious greeting, Copeland was snarling at her.

"Get the hell out of here, Rosalie."

"You guys busy?" she said, ignoring him. "Did you get a match on the prints you pulled from Duncan's place? Matches to the murder weapon?"

Copeland didn't respond. He jerked his chin at Detective Delaney-Carson and she nodded. She left the room, Copeland followed with little more than a glare in Rosalie's direction.

She waited until both detectives were out of the room, then turned to Hart, who was sitting at a desk. Expressly not making eye contact with her.

"Where are they going?"

He studied her with that pinched-cop look she hated. Especially from Hart, because unlike Copeland, he had an excellent bedside manner. Which meant it felt like he was *pitying* her, and she'd rather spar with Copeland than be *pitied* or treated gently by her cousin's husband.

"There's movement on the case," Hart said with careful *cop* language.

"What kind of movement?"

"The kind I can give you a general debrief on, because you'll find out soon enough once you talk to the Kirks. But I need you to promise to keep clear of it for a little bit while we sort out some logistics."

"Why would I promise that?"

"Because otherwise I'll make you go get the information out of the Kirks. I know I can't stop you, Rosalie, but I can slow you down."

She scowled, but figured he would do just that, and she didn't want to be slowed down because there was movement. Besides, she didn't have to keep any promises. Not if it meant helping.

"I know you'll keep your word if you promise, Rosalie," Hart said gravely and seriously.

Oh, damn him and his guilt tactics. "Fine, I promise I won't get in the way *this* morning. So just tell me."

"We didn't get a match on the prints in Duncan's place yet. We're still waiting on the report for the murder weapon too. It's a process, full of red tape. You know this."

"Yeah, I do. So, what's the movement then?"

"There was an emergency call out at the bunks at the Kirk Ranch not too long ago. One of their hands was unresponsive, had clearly taken a large number of pills. Ambulance got out there and transported the patient to Bent County Hospital."

Oh God. Pills. It had to be Duncan's pills. It just had to be. One of the ranch hands had… "Owen." He'd been so distraught over Hunter. It made the most sense that it was Owen who'd done it.

Hart's expression was grim. "What I can confirm is

Owen Green was transported to Bent County Hospital. The first responders confiscated the remaining pills they found on the scene, and we can confirm they are the same type of pills Duncan Kirk reported stolen last night."

Owen had stolen Duncan's pills. Trashed his cabin. But why? Just to hurt himself? She might have believed that if he hadn't made a mess of Duncan's whole place. That he'd just been looking for oblivion.

But the scene of the crime didn't make sense if all he wanted was some pills. There were other ways to get drugs around here, no doubt. It just didn't add up, and worse, it made her heart hurt, the whole of it. She rubbed at her chest, trying to determine her next move. "But... Owen's alive?"

"So far. We haven't been notified of a change in his condition. We will be, either way, and if he wakes up, we'll need to question him on the pills."

She hated the thought of it. Of Owen stealing from Duncan. Making that mess in the cabin. She just hated all of this. She really hadn't pegged him as capable of it.

"Rosalie, I know you're close with the Kirks, and I'm not sure they realize what the next step of this is going to be."

For a minute, she was confused. But it connected, and quickly, just what the next steps the detectives would need to take.

They were going to try to connect Owen to Hunter's murder. Because how could the burglary, the murder, and a suicide attempt in this short of time on the same ranch not connect?

"I need you to let us do our job, Rosalie," Hart said, trotting out his no-nonsense detective voice that brooked no argument. "Trust us to do our job. You're a hell of an investigator, but this is a big deal, and we need to make certain our case doesn't have any inconsistencies."

"Owen didn't kill Hunter, Thomas. Hunter was his friend." All she could think about was him crying at that table in the bunkhouse. Maybe it was guilt. Maybe a response to killing, but...

She just couldn't believe it of him.

"Unfortunately, when you add drugs to the equation, nothing is as cut-and-dried as *friend*," Hart said gently. "But if there's no evidence he did it, then that's going to tie our hands."

Rosalie wanted to argue with Hart about drugs and murder, but what was the point? Hart was right. Drugs complicated everything, and both Owen and Hunter had a history of being involved in them.

But that didn't make Owen a murderer. And there was no evidence, so... "You're still waiting on the reports for the Kirk weapons Copeland confiscated?"

Hart nodded. "Yes. Looks to be a few more days yet."

Slow and frustrating. "Do you know if the Kirks are at the hospital?"

"I'm going to ask you to stay away from the hospital."

She shook her head. "No go, Thomas. If they're there, I'm going to stop by and make sure they're taking care of themselves."

"If I thought that's all you'd do, I'd be okay with it. But I know you, Rosalie. You're going to try to push your way into Owen's room, and if he's awake at all, you're going to try to push your way into our investigation."

"I'm a licensed investigator. What I find out will hold up in court."

"You're too close to this case. You're a liability. Stay away from the hospital. Okay? Don't put me in an awkward position at home."

More guilt. She wanted to hate him for it, but how could

she? The fact he was even being kind about this was because he was married to her cousin. Otherwise he'd tell her to get lost and threaten to arrest her if she went to that hospital.

But she didn't need to go to the hospital to help. "Fine," she muttered. "Can you at least let me know if he wakes up?"

"I'm sure the Kirks will."

She wanted to roll her eyes, but instead she just left the office without so much as a thanks or goodbye.

Halfway through the parking lot on the way to her car, her phone rang. She pulled it out of her pocket.

Duncan.

She closed her eyes, took a deep breath. Answered.

"Hey," he said, his voice sounding rough and tired. She wondered how much sleep he'd gotten. "I've got some… alarming news."

"I'm at the police station, so I just heard. What can I do?"

"Mom and Terry are at the hospital with Owen. I convinced Dad to stay behind, but he's distraught. It's a hell of a mess."

"Yeah, it is." And she couldn't break it to him that the detectives were going to lean on the Owen theory now. But there were things they could do. She *was* an investigator, and if Hart was so dead set on keeping her away from the hospital, she'd take another angle. "I'm coming out."

"You don't have—"

"I'm coming out so we can do some investigating of our own. Can your dad clear out the bunkhouse for a bit?"

Duncan was quiet for a minute. "I imagine everyone will be getting back to work soon enough."

"Good. Meet me by the bunkhouse. Make sure it's empty." She was going to find *something* to prove that Owen hadn't killed his friend.

Chapter Fifteen

Duncan couldn't remember the last time he'd felt so god-awful, but he looked at his father and knew that he'd suffer through a hundred days more of his god-awful if he could take even one weight off his father's shoulders.

He'd forced Dad to eat some breakfast, drink some coffee, then walked down to the stables with him. He tried to think of something to make small talk about, but every topic Dad cared about felt like a minefield.

Mom was better at this kind of thing, but she was also better at hospitals. At logistics. So waiting for Owen's prognosis there with Terry made more sense, but that didn't magically allow Duncan access to the tricks of the trade to keep Dad busy.

They were walking the fence line between the Young Ranch and Kirk property, checking out gate locks, when Duncan's phone chimed. A text from Mom. He read it then relayed the information to Dad.

"Owen's stable. He'll be all right."

Dad nodded slowly, took a few more steps, then came to a stop. He rested an elbow on the fence post and looked over the ranch that stretched out in front of him.

"I called his grandmother. My cousin." He looked so damn grave, Duncan didn't know what to say to that. "You know, I don't take those kids because their parents want them out of trouble," Dad said, staring at the horizon. "I think if that's all it was, your mother would put her foot down. But she knows, I took those kids because their parents don't care about their trouble, and someone should."

Duncan stared at his father for a full minute in absolute stunned silence. He'd never considered... He always assumed Dad's relatives called him up and begged them to fix their kids, and because Dad was a softie, deep down, he couldn't say no.

It had never occurred to Duncan that Dad took it upon himself to help.

And it should have, he realized here in this quiet moment. Mom handling Hunter's funeral should have made it clear to him. These *cousins*, or friends of cousins, or whoever Dad had taken in over the years hadn't needed straightening out so much as a soft place to land.

And Dad had found a way to give that to them. Completely and selflessly, simply because he couldn't stand the idea that someone wasn't cared for.

"I called his grandmother," Dad continued. "My own cousin. We used to spend summers together right here, the lot of us running around while my grandmother and grandfather kept us whole and busy and *loved*. I called his own damn grandmother, and she... She basically said it was the boy's own choice. Like he ever had a choice with parents who didn't care. Grandparents who didn't care." Dad shook his head, and Duncan didn't know that he'd ever seen his father so upset, except maybe at his own mother's funeral.

"That boy could have died, and not her nor his parents gave half a damn. Despicable, is what it is. Far worse than anything Owen's gotten himself messed up in."

Duncan had always known his dad was probably the

best man he knew, but he'd never actually *thought* about it. Comprehended what that meant.

And now that he had, he had to say *something*. "I hope you both know how much I appreciate you. The both of you. Everything you sacrificed for me over the years. I've never thanked you, but I've always appreciated it."

Dad grunted, shifted from foot to foot, clearly uncomfortable with the gratitude and naked emotion. Which Duncan supposed was why he'd never vocalized it before.

Dad squinted, shaded his eyes. "Looks like Rosalie's truck is coming on up," he said, not engaging with Duncan's comment at all.

"She wants to take a look through the bunks. I don't imagine you could make sure no one comes back while we do that?"

Dad nodded grimly. "I'll make sure. Everyone's out, either in the south or north pasture, and Terry is at the hospital. I'll keep an eye out for anybody returning and give you a call if I see someone headed that way."

"Thanks." He hesitated a minute, because leaving Dad alone seemed like a bad idea.

"You go on. I want to get to the bottom of this, before another boy winds up dead or this close to it. You go on up and meet her there. I won't crumble apart."

"No, you never have." So Duncan couldn't allow himself to either. Duncan patted his father on the shoulder, then walked toward Rosalie's approaching truck. They'd get to the bottom of it. If anyone could, it was Rosalie.

Once he reached the truck, she rolled down the window and leaned out, so he headed to the driver's side.

"Hop in," she greeted. "I'm going to park down at your cabin. Then walk up to the bunks. The less chance of someone noticing me poking around the bunkhouse, the better."

It was a good thought, so Duncan followed her instructions. He climbed into the passenger seat, then looked over at her as she drove. She'd put on a little makeup, but he figured it was just to hide how tired she looked.

She pulled to a stop in front of his cabin, but he didn't get out right away. He reached across the center console, swept his thumb under her eye. "You ever going to sleep, Red?"

She studied him for a minute, neither of them leaning into the touch or away from it. Almost sizing it up, deciding what to do about it. But she didn't react either way. Just kept still and fixed him with her own stern look.

Which was a lot different than *last night*. Before everything had gone off the rails. But he thought of his dad, torn up about Owen and the people who didn't care about him, and knew he needed to focus on getting to the bottom of this.

Not figuring out him and Rosalie.

"You ever going to not be in pain, Ace?" she finally asked him after all those beats of silence.

He sighed in spite of himself, dropped his hand, and rotated his bad arm a little. "Feels like the answer is no, but it just takes time. The pharmacy said it might be a day or two before they can get the prescription filled."

"You're telling me a millionaire can't get himself some pain pills before a few days?"

He scowled a little, because there probably were strings he could have pulled, but he didn't like pulling them here. It felt…embarrassing.

"I'll be just fine."

"No doubt. You need your sling? Something to take the edge off?"

He glared at her. "You babying me?"

"If you need babying, look somewhere else."

"Yeah, you like to pretend you're real tough, Rosalie, but you know what's clear to me?"

"What?"

"You're a big old softie."

She snorted. "You're a little delusional there, Ace," she said, hopping out of the truck before he could reply.

But he knew he wasn't. There were people she had a soft spot for, and somehow, he happened to be one of them. It didn't hurt his ego any that she seemed frustrated about it or in denial about it. She'd get over it at some point.

But first, they had some mysteries to solve.

THEY WALKED UP to the bunkhouse. Rosalie considered bringing up last night. Laying down some ground rules. Like maybe that it was a one-off.

But she knew she'd be lying to herself and him if she said any of that, and since now wasn't the time or place to try to dig into a lie—especially after the *softie* accusation—she decided not to mention it at all.

And if she was irritated *he* didn't bring it up, didn't even mention it or try to pursue a line of conversation about it, well… She'd deal with that later. When he wasn't accusing her of being a *softie*.

It grated for a wide variety of reasons because it was both untrue and…true. When it came to certain people, she couldn't keep her defenses up and hard outer shell in place. Certain people, like *all men*, had always been easy to harden herself against.

But she couldn't seem to manage with Duncan.

Which was going to get her hurt, and she knew it. So she wanted to *avoid* it because she wasn't a masochist.

Apparently, except when it came to him.

He didn't try to make conversation on the walk over to

the bunkhouse, and she told herself she was grateful for it. Silence was great for thinking, and she needed to be thinking about what she was looking for.

Something… *Something*. Anything that might give her even half an idea to go on. Because this was just getting more and more confusing as more terrible things happened.

Duncan unlocked the front door and gestured her inside. She'd been in this room before, when they'd talked to Owen the day of the murder. So, that wasn't what she'd come for today. "You know which room is Owen's?"

"No, but I might be able to figure it out." He moved through the common area, back to a long hallway with lots of doors. Only one of them was open. Duncan gestured to it. "This would be my guess."

Rosalie brushed past him and stepped inside. It was in disarray. There were muddy boot prints from more than one person—probably the paramedics and cops. So, yeah, Owen's room. There were two beds in it—one on either side. "Did he share a room?"

"Not sure, but I can find out."

"Probably with Hunter, if he did," she said, more to herself than to Duncan, trying to get in the right frame of mind. Because investigating was her job, and she was damn good at it. She'd searched plenty of rooms before. She'd found evidence of theft, affairs, abuse.

She had to keep an open and agile mind. She had to think like the person she was investigating.

"What exactly are you looking for?" Duncan asked.

"I'm not sure. The police confiscated the pills. I'm sure they searched the area. Took pictures of what they found so they can connect it to your case. I don't know that I can magically unearth something they didn't, but I want to look. Get a sense of things." She pulled a pair of latex gloves out of the cross-body bag strapped to her chest and began to pull them on.

Since Duncan was giving her a funny look, she gestured around the room. "Don't touch anything. The police might come back to take prints, like they did at your place."

"Fingerprints," Duncan said, frowning. "Right."

"Having second thoughts, Ace?"

He sighed. "No, but I can't say that means I'm comfortable with all this."

"You can always leave me to it."

He shook his head, but he stayed there, hovering closer to the door than anything else. Rosalie started on one side of the room. She studied walls, baseboards, furniture. There wasn't much. Even the little closet just housed some clothes, a few pairs of boots, and little else. Nothing really personal.

It made her feel even more sorry for Owen in the hospital. Hunter, dead without ever having a chance to have a life that was more than this…impersonal holding pattern. She went through a nightstand, but it was empty. Hunter's likely, because the police would have confiscated any of his personal effects for their investigation.

She moved to the next nightstand and found more items in there. A few receipts—from a gas-station convenience store for what looked like a fountain drink and some snacks, a Rightful Claim bar tab from before Hunter's murder, and some fishing bait. Nothing that stuck out as important, but she made sure to commit it all to memory so she could transfer it to her notes later.

There was a book under the receipts. A bible. Suspicious, Rosalie lifted it out of the drawer, flipped through it, then held it over the bed, pages down, and shook.

A little square of paper tumbled out of the book and onto

the bed. Rosalie set aside the bible, picked up the paper, and began to carefully unfold it.

It was a map of the ranch. Boundaries were marked, and there were little hash marks where the different cattle herds were.

It was similar to the one Duncan's mother had made, but not identical. Which meant it was Owen's own map, outlining exactly what Rosalie had wanted outlined to see if they could connect the murder to the missing cattle.

Rosalie's heart sank. She shouldn't have any feelings about it, but she felt…bad. Bad for poor Owen. Bad for Hunter. Just a bad sign that maybe, just maybe, all her instincts about this case were wrong.

She moved over to Duncan and showed it to him. His expression went very hard.

"That doesn't look too good for Owen, does it?"

She shook her head. "No, it doesn't look good." She looked around this little room. Why would he have this? Why would he have anything to do with the cattle? Murder was one thing, but the missing cattle?

But then again, why would he steal Duncan's pills and take most of them himself? There were a lot of ways to hurt yourself when you were distraught. Stealing Duncan's pills had required quite a bit of effort. None of the answers to any of those questions made much sense.

"Are you going to take that to the cops?" Duncan asked, not showing any emotion regarding how he might feel about either answer.

She should take it straight to the cops, or even just call Copeland to come out. She wasn't even concerned about explaining how she'd come across it. She was a private investigator with the landowner's permission to search. She had Duncan as an eyewitness.

But… "I don't like this. Something doesn't feel right." Still, she refolded the paper, then slid it into a little evidence container she'd put in her bag. Then slid both into the bag. "Let's search the rest before we decide what to do with it." She moved past him and back into the hall. She went through room after room. Some guys had more items than others, some more personal than others, like they'd made this their home, their life.

But nothing that seemed to connect to the missing cattle, the murder, or the pills. She reached the final room at the end of the hall, but before she could reach for the knob, Duncan stopped her.

"That's the one room I know who it belongs to. It's Terry's room. I don't know how I feel about his privacy being violated. Owen is one thing, but you're talking about the guy who's been my dad's right-hand man for over a decade."

"If it offends your sensibilities, go away. I'm finishing the job."

He scowled, but he also moved out of the way.

Rosalie tried to turn the knob, but it didn't open. "It's locked."

"Makes sense. Each room is each man's living quarters. It's private."

Rosalie rolled her eyes at the censure in his tone. "No one else had theirs locked. And if he's innocent, what does it matter? Avert your eyes, Ace, I'm about to break the law."

This wouldn't be admissible in a court of law, but if it gave her something to go on, to investigate, she could do that. She would do that. She pulled her keychain out of her pocket, assessed which tool would be best, then stuck it into the keyhole.

After a few minutes of teasing it out, she finally managed to unlock the door and push it open. She didn't look back at Duncan to see how he felt about it. It didn't matter.

She expected Terry's room to be more…cluttered. He'd been here the longest. A long, long time. A man in his fifties, no doubt planning to stay.

But it was…a lot like Owen's. Sparse. Not personal. There were no pictures, no knickknacks, no books. Just clothes and hats, a few toiletries, and some notebooks and pens on a tiny desk.

She flipped through them. All blank.

Rosalie really didn't know what to make of it. "Why doesn't Terry live in the cabin you're in? Back when we had a full crew, our foreman lived in his own place, separate from the bunkhouse. A pecking-order kind of thing."

"Dad offered years ago when Terry got the promotion. Terry declined. Said he preferred to live with the men he was leading."

A good sentiment for a foreman to have. It showed a loyalty she was no doubt not repaying by poking around his things. But still, something…prickled at her neck. A kind of investigative sixth sense, but she couldn't find the center of it, the reason for it.

What was she missing here?

Duncan's phone chimed, interrupting her thoughts. She looked over at him as he studied the screen.

"It's Dad. A couple hands are on their way back. They'll stop with their horses at the stables first, but we better get out of here if we're wanting to keep this on the DL."

Rosalie gave one last quick look around. Nothing. Nothing stuck out to her, and the police would have searched the entire bunkhouse after Hunter's murder. She was just… desperate for answers, sadly.

She pulled off the gloves as they walked out of the bunkhouse. She shoved them into her back pocket. She blinked against the bright afternoon sky, as she walked side by side with Duncan back to his cabin.

"So what's next?"

Rosalie knew the answer, but that didn't mean she liked it. "I guess I'm going to take that map to the cops."

"You don't want to."

"No, I don't. Something about this doesn't feel like the whole story. But unfortunately, without police help, I don't think we can find the whole story." She didn't say the rest of what she thought: She wasn't even sure they'd find it *with* police help.

"Let me grab my keys."

"You don't have to come, Duncan. I can—"

"Let me grab my keys," he repeated firmly, striding over to his door.

She could leave without him. Handle this on her own. She didn't need a partner. She didn't need his input.

But she waited for him all the same.

Chapter Sixteen

Duncan wasn't surprised to be met with Detective Beckett's creatively crude curses when Rosalie strode into the little office the detectives shared.

Because the man who'd been introduced as Hart was standing in a corner—he also wasn't wearing his sling anymore. Then there was a woman. Blond and blue-eyed, dressed in slacks and a Bent County polo shirt. Midthirties, or maybe pushing forty. Cop, *clearly*, so maybe a third detective. She looked vaguely familiar, but Duncan couldn't place her and didn't have the energy to try.

"We're too busy to deal with you two," Detective Beckett said disgustedly.

"And apparently too busy to do your job," Rosalie returned, none of that fake cheer she usually used on Beckett. She was just straight pissed.

She slapped the bag with the map in it on the desk. "I found that in Owen Green's bible."

"Don't BS me, Rosalie," Beckett said disgustedly. "There was nothing in that damn bible, and what the hell were you doing poking around Owen Green's room?"

Since Duncan didn't care for this guy's entire demeanor, he waded in. "She had the property owner's permission."

Detective Beckett's angry gaze moved to Duncan. "Last time I checked you weren't the property owner."

"Yeah, but my father is. He knew. He was okay with it. You can verify that."

"Your parents should reconsider just who they're so free and easy with giving permissions to," Beckett replied.

"Why don't we all take a breath," the female detective said, pushing into a standing position from behind the desk. "I understand this is stressful and heated. We have an unsolved murder, a burglary, and a suicide attempt. This is serious, but sniping at each other certainly doesn't solve anything."

"My case," Beckett said, crossing his arms over his chest and continuing to glare at Rosalie. "I like sniping."

"Your case, your screwup," Rosalie retorted. "That map was in that bible. You didn't search it hard enough," Rosalie insisted, clearly ignoring the other detective.

"You can make a stink all you want, but you're not a cop. You're not a detective. Go private investigate all you want, but this is my case, and I don't need you screwing it up with lies brought on by whatever this is," he said, gesturing at Duncan. "I searched that bible. I've got bodycam footage to prove my point—not that I need to prove it to *you*."

Bodycam footage. Duncan frowned. Beckett had to be lying. It didn't make any sense otherwise. "I watched her do it," Duncan said. "I watched her upend the bible and the map fell out. It happened. So explain that with your bodycam."

The detectives somehow all shared a look. A beat of silence.

"It wasn't there this morning," Detective Beckett said, sounding more in control of his irritation. More concerned and considering than offended now. "Not only did I shake out the bible, I flipped through every page. There's not a stone I didn't turn over in that room. So if it was there *after...*"

"Someone *else* put it there," Rosalie said, finishing for him.

Duncan didn't like that *if* still hanging out in Beckett's sentence, but Rosalie didn't seem offended. Like Beckett, she seemed to have turned frustration and irritation into concern with the case at the drop of the hat.

It was enough to give a normal guy emotional whiplash.

"Which means that map isn't Owen Green's and he didn't put it there," Rosalie said. "Because Owen was in the hospital in between the police search and mine."

Even with the whiplash, Duncan kept up. "So was Terry. Terry Boothe, our foreman," Duncan clarified for the detectives, though they probably knew all the players. "He went with my mother to the hospital to wait on word about Owen's prognosis after the ambulance left."

Detective Beckett nodded thoughtfully. "I guess that's three people we can mark off the list. Who else has access to the bunkhouse?"

"It'd be the same list we gave you after Hunter's murder. Nothing would have changed."

"No. Nothing would have changed," Beckett agreed, but his gaze of suspicion was pinned on Duncan. "I don't recall your name being on that list."

Duncan blinked in surprised. "*My* name?"

"You have access to that bunkhouse, right?" Beckett asked, sounding somehow casual and deadly serious all at the same time.

Accusing him. Him. When he'd had his place trashed, his painkillers stolen. The detective was standing there throwing suspicion on him? "Yeah, I've got access," Duncan replied, anger coursing through him.

Detective Beckett shrugged casually. "Seems to me you're the new person in all this. You own any guns you haven't told us about, Mr. Kirk?"

It was…absolutely ludicrous. Duncan had never been a guy with much of a temper. All his feelings, all his passion, had always been centered on baseball.

But something hot and dangerous erupted inside of him now. He took a step toward Beckett. "Seems to me—"

But Rosalie grabbed his arm—his bad arm—and squeezed. Hard enough he couldn't get a word out because pain zinged through him.

"See if you can get some prints off that map," she said, interrupting whatever else Duncan might have said.

"You don't run this investigation, Rosalie. And you might consider your partner a liability until you know for sure…"

But Rosalie was dragging Duncan out of the office, and he didn't hear the rest of the detective's sentence.

"Look, I get that you're pissed and you have every right to be," she said in a low, seething voice, still pulling him along by his bad arm. "But if you assault an officer of the law, we'll have big problems. Let's cool off somewhere we're not so likely to get arrested for assault."

"We?" he demanded. Because she seemed a hell of a lot more in control of herself than he felt of himself.

"Yeah, *we*. Accusing you is a jerk move for no good reason except to get a rise. We won't give him what he wants. So we walk away before we start swinging."

The idea of her starting to swing, the picture of it in his head, was enough to soothe some of the roiling anger. But that didn't make this something he could swallow.

"How do you do all this?" he asked as they strode out of the police department and into the sunny afternoon.

"All what?" she asked, still moving at a quick pace toward her truck.

"Deal with an ego like that?"

"You know what's funny? I'd bet money on the fact that back in that little office of theirs, they're having a conversation about how they handle dealing with me and my ego."

Duncan didn't have a quick retort to that, because he imagined it was true. He just didn't happen to find Rosalie's ego damn insulting.

They reached her truck, but Rosalie didn't unlock the doors. She stood at the bed and sighed, squinting up at the sky. "Bottom line? We're all good at our jobs. We all want the same things. But we have to go at it in different ways. Which means we butt heads and things get heated. Outside that heat, I can tell you, Copeland and I are a little too much alike and that's probably half our problem." She wrinkled her nose. "I'd have done the same in his position—needle you, see what came out. As little as I like to admit that we go about things the same way, we do."

"That's very diplomatic of you," Duncan replied, because even if some of his anger had cooled, he didn't feel like being fair or diplomatic when it came to Detective Beckett.

"Yeah, well, if I couldn't find that diplomacy deep down on occasion, I'd have been arrested a long time ago." She smiled at him, but it wasn't her usual flash of personality. There was something sad behind it.

Because they could be annoyed at Beckett or the detectives, or any number of things, but it didn't change the very clear facts of the matter.

"Someone on that ranch is the problem," Duncan said quietly.

"Yeah."

A problem. A murderer. Someone who had access to Owen's room. Someone right under his parents' nose had killed a man. And was trying to make Owen look responsible. It didn't feel like trouble brought with them. It felt like trouble right there in his home.

"Whoever killed Hunter wants Owen to look guilty. Wants to tie the whole thing to these damn missing cows, or that map wouldn't have been planted. But that was their first mistake. Planting that map *after* the detectives means we *know* there's a frame job happening."

"No one knows you looked today," Duncan said. "Not yet."

Rosalie seemed to consider that. "So who were they hoping *would* look? And when? Did they think the detectives were coming back?" She shook her head. "More questions and no more answers."

"That isn't true. We can cross Owen off any suspect list."

"Except your burglary," Rosalie said. "Unless… What if he didn't steal those pills? What if he didn't voluntarily take those pills?"

"Is that a leap?"

"Maybe. But it's one I want to look into. The fact of the matter is someone was already murdered. Whoever was behind that isn't above hurting people, so it isn't a leap to wonder if they forced Owen to take those pills. To frame him for all of this."

Duncan wasn't sure. This all felt like a stretch, but it was reality. A dead ranch hand. Stolen pills. Missing cattle. "Too bad we don't have a security camera on the bunkhouse."

Rosalie clapped her hands. "But we can. We absolutely can, and no one has to know."

ROSALIE DROVE WITH more determination than caution, and though Duncan didn't outwardly react, she didn't miss the way his good hand gripped the door like it would save him.

She supposed it made her a bad person, but it amused her. So she didn't slow down. She drove fast and only a *little* recklessly to Fool's Gold headquarters.

Because these little things that didn't add up were all steps. Maybe she couldn't see the top of the staircase yet, but she was building it.

She parked in her spot behind Fool's Gold HQ. She noted there were a couple of vehicles in the lot. Quinn's truck, and a car she didn't recognize. Brand-new, it seemed.

"We've got a lot of surveillance equipment. I'll grab what I want, and then we'll head out to the ranch. Do you think everyone will be out of the bunks tomorrow morning?"

"What about tonight?"

"I can put the outside surveillance up tonight without raising any eyebrows, but I don't think I can get anything inside as long as people are there. We'll just have to chance giving it some time. This only works if no one knows we're on to them."

Rosalie unlocked the back door, gestured Duncan inside, then led him down the little hall toward the equipment room. She heard voices, so she popped her head into the main office area where Quinn was standing with Anna Hudson-Steele, who wasn't working, considering she had her toddler on her hip.

They both looked over at her, or probably at Duncan hovering behind her.

"Just came in to pick up some surveillance equipment. Anna. That your new car out there?"

"Yeah. Had to upgrade." She patted her stomach. "And be relegated to desk duty again for a while."

"Aw. Congratulations. You and Hawk make cute babies."

"That we do. That your new partner back there?" Anna asked, eyeing Duncan.

Rosalie didn't scowl, though she wanted to. "Anna, this is Duncan. Duncan, Anna's one of our part-time investigators. You probably know some of her older siblings. She's a Hudson."

"Guilty as charged," Anna said with a grin, bouncing the toddler on her hip. "I heard you're having problems out at your folks' ranch. You have our sympathy there, but Rosalie'll get to the bottom of it. Stubborn is her middle name."

"Pot. Kettle."

"I have mellowed in my old age and motherhood era," Anna replied loftily.

"My butt," Quinn muttered, making Anna laugh.

"Well, congrats again. But we've got to get to work." Since Duncan was right behind her, and there wasn't room to move in this tight part of the hallway, she pointed down the hall. "Door at the end."

Before she could follow him, Anna called out.

"Hey, Rosalie?"

Rosalie popped her head back in. Anna pointed out where Duncan had gone down the hall, then pretended to fan herself, and Rosalie rolled her eyes and walked away, amused in spite of herself.

She went down to the storage room, unlocked it and led Duncan inside. Duncan was quiet and frowning, clearly working something over in his head while Rosalie gathered what she thought she'd need.

"What's on your mind, Ace?" she asked once she was sure she had everything.

"The Hudsons. Their parents went missing all those years ago. For years, no one knew what happened."

She studied him for a minute. Worry. But it wasn't for himself, or even the truth. He was worried about his parents dealing with unknowns for years, and she couldn't give him a hard time for that, or let it stand. "Yeah. But there were no bodies. They disappeared. It's different, Duncan. We're going to get to the bottom of this."

His gaze moved from the door to her. "Because stubborn is your middle name?"

"Because, as little as it might seem right now, we've got plenty to go on. So let's get on it." They walked back out to her truck, and she drove to the Kirk Ranch with her radio on, trying to discourage conversation.

She needed to think. About camera placement. About how to untangle these strange twists and turns.

About literally anything but *him*.

It was dark when they arrived back at the Kirks', which was good because she'd need dark to hide a surveillance camera outside the bunkhouse. She parked down at his cabin again. People would just think…

Well, she didn't need to consider that. "You can stay here," she told Duncan, maybe a little tersely, as she hopped out. She opened the back door of the truck, pulled out the equipment she'd need for an outdoor camera placement.

He came over to her side of the truck.

"I'm going with you."

"Look, it'll take maybe fifteen minutes when I get up

there, and it's less suspicious or noticeable if it's just me wandering around in the dark."

"That's a lie and you know it."

She stopped what she was doing and glared at him, though it didn't matter. It was dark and the light on his porch didn't reach all the way out here.

"You're not wandering around in the dark with an unknown murderer on the loose, Rosalie."

"Because you're going to save me with your wounded arm even though I'm the one carrying?"

He sighed at her. "Because you'll be focused on putting up the camera, and you need someone watching out to make sure no one happens upon you doing it."

She couldn't argue with that, even though she wanted to. But she was being prickly and petty for no good reason, and that irritated her too.

So she let him tag along. They crept across the ranch in the dark, and Rosalie was used to this kind of thing, but Duncan must have still known the ranch pretty well despite all his time away because he didn't take any stumbles or make any noise.

There were a few old trees around the bunkhouse, and Rosalie had already decided on hooking her camera up to the one that faced the front door. If anyone noticed it, it could easily be played off as a trail camera meant to catch glimpses of wildlife, not people.

"I've got to use some light, so situate yourself in front of me where your body should block most of it from anyone looking out from the bunkhouse. But make sure you've got a good view of the door and the driveway."

Duncan followed instructions, but unfortunately, he was right. With his eyes watching, she could focus on the work rather than worrying if anyone was spotting her. She wished she could get into that bunkhouse, hide a few cameras in strategic places, but she had to believe tomorrow morning would be soon enough.

What would happen in there tonight with Owen in the hospital? She didn't think much of anything. She hoped to God nothing.

Once she was sure the camera was connected and she could access it from her phone, she tapped Duncan on the shoulder. "Good," she whispered.

They didn't say anything, just started walking back to his cabin. Once they were closer to his cabin than the bunkhouse, Duncan spoke.

"What about actual surveillance? Like following guys around? Watching what they do?"

"Even if you hired out all of Fool's Gold, we wouldn't be able to follow everyone. Maybe if we just watched who came and went, but even that's a tall order considering most of these guys only leave the ranch sporadically."

"Well, we don't have to follow Terry. Maybe we can do it like that. Narrow down who it could have been."

Rosalie nodded. "See if your dad knows where everyone was over the course of the morning. Anything we can rule out helps us focus in."

"He'll be in bed by now, and he hasn't been sleeping, so I don't want to interrupt on the off chance he is. I'll talk to him in the morning, see what he can tell me. Maybe talk to Terry. Even if he was at the hospital all morning, he would know what everyone was supposed to be working on."

"Good idea. I know Terry's not on our list, but we need to be careful what we tell him, so he doesn't inadvertently let on to whoever is doing this something we don't want spread around. No matter who we think is innocent, we have to be careful what we say to them."

"That's depressing."

"That's murder investigations for you."

He didn't say anything to that as they approached his yard. But before she could break away and head for her truck, he grabbed her hand.

"I'm sure I've got leftovers in my fridge. Come in and eat some dinner."

She studied the cabin. There was one light on inside, the porch light beaming at them like some sort of welcoming beacon.

Last night, she'd said yes. This morning she'd snuck out of his bed, and out of his cabin, without anything having happened last night. They hadn't spoken about it all day. Hadn't acknowledged it in any way. They'd focused on what was important.

She'd been given a reprieve. Time to screw her head back on and not be dazzled by him. She needed to take that save.

"I better not." She pulled her hand out of his. "I'll see you around, Ace."

He frowned at her, but she turned away from him. Started walking to her truck. The sensible thing was to cut this off at the pass while she still could. If they focused on this case, then they didn't have to deal with whatever aberration last night had been.

It was the smart, sensible, *safe* thing. And maybe that wasn't her usual MO, but it had to be when it came to Duncan Kirk.

"Hey."

"Hey what?" she asked, turning around. She'd barely gotten the *what* out of her mouth when his lips touched hers. His good arm wrapped around her waist, pulling her close and into this… *Vortex* was the only word for it, because everything else disappeared.

Over the course of the day, focusing on work and not mentioning last night at all, she'd almost convinced herself that the memory of kissing him was an exaggeration.

But it wasn't. Nothing could be. She didn't understand how one man could kiss her in a way that made every other kiss that came before stupid and pointless. Weak and pitiful compared to this wallop of a sensation. His mouth on hers, his arms around her. A *vortex* she couldn't fight.

Didn't want to, damn it.

He eased his mouth from hers, but he didn't let her go. His gaze was direct and intent. "This murder mess may take precedence, but this isn't going away. *I'm* not going away."

Rosalie found herself utterly and uncharacteristically speechless. Her heart hammered, and it wasn't just the kiss. The chemistry. It was the way he looked at her that seemed to unearth her foundations she thought were so steady.

He ruined them so damn easily. Made her want to melt when she knew all the disastrous ways believing in someone ended.

"Still going home?" he asked, one eyebrow raised.

She should, just to prove that she could. She should, because she was a smart woman who knew how to guard her damn soft heart.

But she shook her head and followed him inside.

Chapter Seventeen

Duncan rolled over to find a naked, sleeping woman in his bed, and figured he could pretend there weren't murderers wandering around for about five minutes to enjoy Rosalie Young sleeping in his bed.

He thought she'd try to sneak out sometime in the night, or early in the morning, like she had the night before. But exhaustion must have caught up with her, because her eyes were closed, her breathing deep and even.

So Duncan slid out of bed, narrowly biting back a hiss at the throbbing pain in his arm. He moved as quietly as he could manage into the kitchen, got the coffee going, then grabbed a banana his mother had no doubt stocked yesterday. He scarfed it down with the express purpose of taking a few ibuprofen with something in his stomach.

He decided to consider it progress that the over-the-counter stuff was helping to take the edge off.

Owen using those pills—or someone using those pills against Owen—really made Duncan reluctant to replace them.

When Rosalie came out of his bedroom, her hair was a mess and she looked bleary-eyed and still half-asleep. She was wearing one of his T-shirts, which nearly went down to her knees.

His heart did one painful roll in his chest, and something inside of him seemed to say "this is it. Right here."

But he hedged on admitting to himself what that *it* was. "Morning, sunshine," he greeted instead.

She just grunted, shuffled over to the coffee maker, saw it hadn't brewed a full cup, then grunted again.

It was amusing to watch. She was usually so put together, so...*vibrant* and in control of herself. She made it look like she was all instinct and wild, but there was a careful note to Rosalie hidden underneath all that bluster.

He liked her bluster. He liked the hint of something softer underneath. He liked her, plain and simple. No doubt if he didn't, it would have been easy enough to let her leave last night.

He wrapped his good arm around her from behind to pull her closer. She stiffened a little, but then she relaxed. It was starting to irritate him. The push and pull. It'd be one thing if she had no interest. If she flat-out rejected him, but she hadn't.

"Look, Duncan..."

Unless she was about to.

"You should probably know, I'm not much of a good bet," she said firmly. Like she'd really been thinking them over and had come to this very clear conclusion.

Except it made no sense.

He couldn't see her expression since he was standing behind her. He could only look down at the top of her head. There were a lot of complexities about Rosalie. No doubt. Hidden things under her brazen surface.

But she was not a woman who suffered from a lack of confidence. So he tried to unearth what she *really* meant by that, but couldn't. Because it just didn't add up. "You're not? Or I'm not?"

She didn't push away from him, and he'd expected her to. It kept his frustration with her in check, that she'd lean against him and have this conversation.

She didn't answer, and he wasn't in the mood to fight, so he figured they could set this aside for now. Get back to murder. Tonight, they could wade through all this.

So he kissed her cheek. "You seem like a pretty good bet from where I'm standing. I'm going to walk up to the main house. See if Dad can come up with a list of anyone who definitely couldn't have been at the bunkhouse between the detectives and us yesterday morning. Shouldn't take too long. You take your time waking up. I'll be back. It'll probably be another hour or two before we can get into the bunks undetected."

He felt her gaze as he released her and walked for the front door. He didn't look back, though he wanted to.

"Duncan?"

Slowly, he turned to face her. Standing in his kitchen, in his shirt, still looking half-asleep and gorgeous.

"Maybe it's not me. Maybe it's the whole…relationship thing. It's a lot of trust. I'm not sure I've got that in me."

He figured it was fair that trust had to be earned, and they had a ways to go on that front. But he was a patient man. A goal-oriented kind of guy. He could prove it, earn it. He would. Not with words. But with the same kind of stubborn tenacity that had led him to success in his career.

"So find it in you, Rosalie. I can wait," he replied, then went ahead and left rather than allow her to keep talking herself out of what they'd already started.

Because they were both people who saw through what they started. She'd come to that conclusion too.

He was *almost* sure of it.

He walked up to his parents' house and let himself in

after a brief tap on the door. They were both in the kitchen eating breakfast. They exchanged a look he didn't quite understand, then smiled at him.

"Morning," Mom offered. "What brings you up?"

"Some questions, unfortunately. Last night Rosalie and I had a bit of a break in the case, I guess you'd say. I need to know who on the ranch might have been unaccounted for between the time the ambulance took Owen away, and the time Rosalie and I looked through the bunkhouse yesterday."

Dad scratched a hand through his hair. "Well. Your mother and Terry were at the hospital. Everyone else would have been doing their assigned job."

"Is there a way to verify they were doing it? Especially if Terry wasn't here?"

Dad seemed to consider this. "Everyone had jobs to do since it's busy season," Dad said. "Terry and I sit down and discuss progress every other day during the busy season— and that's where he'd mention if someone was slacking off or something didn't get done. We didn't last night with the hospital hubbub. I can try to pin him down this morning. Get a rundown of yesterday."

"That'd be good." Would it give them answers? Before he could say anything else to Dad, his phone chimed. Duncan pulled it out of his pocket and read the text from Rosalie.

Owen's awake. Headed to the hospital to talk to him. Text after.

The phone on the wall rang, and Mom got up to answer. Duncan could tell by her reactions that she was getting the same information that Rosalie had just texted him.

She hung up then smiled over at him. "Owen's awake,

and Sharon thinks she can get me in to see him today. So I'm going to head up to the hospital. I know Terry is worried sick about that boy. I'm going to call down and see if he wants to ride together this time."

Duncan nodded but before his mother could lift the receiver again, the words caught up in his head. "This time? You two didn't ride together yesterday?" he demanded.

"No, Terry wanted to make sure everything was settled before he left. He couldn't have been more than twenty minutes behind me though. Waited all day with me too. But they wouldn't let us see Owen. Hopefully today."

"Yeah, hopefully." Duncan kept the smile in place and rejected the awful thought that wanted to take root. Sure, it gave Terry time to plant the map, but why would he? There was no reason. Not that anyone else had a reason. But the point was, anyone could have put that map there.

Anyone, including Terry.

Mom made the call, but Terry didn't answer. "Must already be out and about. I'll text his cell. You probably have things to handle this morning, Duncan," she said to him. She moved for the counter. "Here. Take some breakfast back with you." Mom handed him a big grocery bag full of food.

He frowned down at the amount. "Mom, this is enough for…"

"Two people?" Mom replied brightly. "I suppose it is. Would you like to discuss that?"

Since he absolutely would *not*, he took it without any other discussion, or mentioning that Rosalie was already leaving, and went back to his cabin.

Once Dad pinned down Terry, got the information on who else might have not done their chores yesterday morning, he'd have a list. A list of suspects. He'd present Rosalie or the detectives with it. It was progress. Steps, like Rosalie said.

And he'd include Terry on that list, even though he didn't want to.

They had to look at every angle, Rosalie had taught him that. So he'd follow every avenue, even when he didn't want to.

ROSALIE PULLED INTO the hospital parking lot. She'd made a quick stop at home for a clean change of clothes and was glad not to run into Audra and have to *explain* everything. Then she drove, faster than she should have, out to the hospital.

Maybe Owen really didn't know anything, but surely he'd remember if someone shoved those pills down his throat. And that was a clearer answer than whatever they *might* find on some cameras set up inside the bunkhouse.

Ideally, though, she'd have time for both. If she hurried.

She screeched into a parking spot and hopped out, plan already in her head. A little fast talking at the nurses' station, but she'd slip into Owen's room without permission if she needed to, a few questions, then…something.

Something.

It was a lot better than thinking about Duncan's parting shot this morning. When she got inside, there was a flurry of activity at the nurses' station. A few discreet questions and she got the gist.

Owen had crashed again. There was a lot of confusion because no one knew why. He'd been in good shape one minute, flatlining the next.

Rosalie wanted to stay and find out what happened, but the hospital hustle reminded her far too much of her father's unexpected death. She'd rather act than sit in *that*.

So she went back to her truck, refused to think about poor Owen crying over his dead friend, and considered her options. No answers from Owen, so she'd have to go back to the ranch and plant her cameras.

Her phone rang as she slid back into her driver's seat. It was Duncan. She thought about ignoring it. About finding some boundaries. When she was at work, she wasn't going to communicate with him.

But her work right now was *him* and his family, and she should probably tell him about Owen. So she answered on speakerphone, so she could drive back to the office while they talked.

"Hey," she answered. "Bad news."

"About Owen? Mom was halfway to the hospital when her friend who works at the hospital called and told her."

"They aren't sure what happened, so I'm headed back to put up those cameras. You got that list from your dad yet?"

"He's talking to everyone now." He paused for a moment. "Rosalie… I don't want to believe this is true. I know my dad doesn't, but… Mom mentioned that she and Terry didn't drive to the hospital together yesterday."

Something cold trickled into Rosalie's bloodstream. A few too many things clicking together with that simple fact. "So when did he?" she asked, careful to keep her tone neutral, even as her heart rate picked up.

"She said he was about twenty minutes behind her, making sure all the jobs were assigned for the day, and maybe he was. He could have been." But Duncan didn't sound convinced.

She found she couldn't argue with him, even though she knew better. There were too many coincidences adding up to Terry being a problem. Maybe not the whole problem, but part of this.

And if he was, everyone at that ranch was in danger, including Duncan. He wouldn't want to go to the cops yet. He wasn't ready to fully believe Terry was the most likely suspect, but she was.

"Listen, Duncan, scratch the cameras. I'm going to head over to Bent County, talk all this through with Copeland," she said. "You stay put with your parents. Keep an eye on everything there. Call if anything seems even remotely fishy, especially with Terry. You have to be careful, even if you want to trust your gut. Okay?"

He sighed. She could just imagine the expression on his face. Frustrated resignation. "Yeah, okay. You be careful too, huh?"

"Sure, that's me."

He chuckled. "Uh-huh. Watch your back, Red. Give me a call when you're done with the detectives."

She should say no. She'd call him when she wanted. She didn't have to *check in* with him. Her job was dangerous, and if he was really so into this and waiting for her to trust him, he'd have to accept that.

But that would inevitably hurt his feelings in this moment, and if she hurt his feelings, she'd be thinking about *that* today, instead of what she needed to be thinking about. Which was how Terry Boothe might be connected to all this.

"I will. 'Bye."

"'Bye."

She ended the call on an irritated sigh. Not sure who or what she was irritated with, except maybe just this clutching, twisting feeling in her chest that was a tangle of feelings she most assuredly didn't want.

But had, for some damn reason.

She drove away from the hospital, which was more centrally located in the county, out north back toward the police station. She heard a faint shuffle of noise behind her. Confused, she turned her head a little to peek in the back. And saw something wholly unexpected.

A gun. Pointed at her head.

Held by the man of the hour, who was sitting up from a crouched position behind her seat.

Terry, who was in the back seat of her truck, with a gun pulled on her. She'd been so distracted by everything happening, she hadn't paid *attention*. He'd been *hiding* back there? For how long?

"Keep driving," Terry ordered.

Rosalie said nothing as her mind whirled. She turned her gaze back to the road, to driving.

Terry had been at the hospital—that was the only time he could have gotten into her truck. *Maybe* at the ranch, but that just didn't add up. He'd been at the hospital.

He'd done something to Owen. *He* was the reason for his crash. He had to be.

"You tried to kill that poor boy. Twice?" She flicked a glance at him in the rearview mirror.

"Drive," he said again. His eyes were flat, his hand on the gun was steady. This was no panicked move. It was planned, and Terry was in charge of himself.

So Rosalie had to be in charge of herself. "Sure. Where are we driving to, boss?"

"You shouldn't have stuck your nose into this. Should have let trash like Hunter Villanova lay. It doesn't give me any joy to do this, but you ruined my plans."

A cold chill snuck up Rosalie's spine. She could handle a gun being pointed in her direction. Maybe it was misplaced confidence, but she figured she was in the driver's seat, so to speak, so she could get out of this.

But Terry having *plans* alarmed her. *Plans* spoke to time putting this all together, whatever this all was. Something she couldn't even begin to guess at. She swallowed her nerves. "What kind of plans, Ter?"

"You're going to turn around at the cut-through here. You're going to drive me back to the Kirk Ranch. And when we get where we're going, you're going to call that boyfriend of yours. I'll spare Norman and Natalie, because it makes sense to. But you two? You've overstayed your welcome."

Rosalie forced herself to laugh even though her throat was dry. "You think you're going to kill Duncan *and* me and get away with it?"

"I don't think I am. I know I am. I've got a plan, and since I know yours, mine'll win out. Go on then. Turn at the cut-through."

Like hell she would. As they came to the cut-through in the highway, Rosalie did everything at once—ducked her head away from the gun, jerked the wheel in the opposite direction toward the ditch instead of the cut-through, and hit the accelerator down to the floor.

When the truck crashed into the ditch, pain exploded in her head, but it wasn't a gunshot, so there was that.

Chapter Eighteen

Duncan hated the roiling feeling of betrayal in his gut. Hated worrying that a man who'd been his father's friend and right-hand man for…forever, really, might have… What? Murdered a kid? Shoved drugs down Owen's mouth?

It didn't make sense.

But nothing else did either. Until Dad came back with a list. Duncan looked at the clock on the oven. It was taking too long. And since Rosalie hadn't called Duncan back, he was going stir-crazy. There had to be something he could *do*.

He'd just walk out to the bunkhouse or stables or wherever Dad was. He'd just walk around until he found *someone* to give him *something* to do.

But when Duncan stepped out of his cabin, he saw Dad walking across the yard. He looked…gray. Not the exhausted pale he'd been dealing with for the past few days, but a kind of wounded gray. Like he was bleeding out from the inside.

"Dad…" Duncan met him at the bottom of the steps, then took him by the arm and led him inside. He pushed him onto the couch, a strange terror jittering through him. Because Dad was *fine*, so it shouldn't be *scary,* but Duncan had never seen his father look quite so weak and old, and it upended the way everything was supposed to be.

"Everyone was accounted for," Dad said, staring at his hands. "Granted, someone could be lying, but Dunc…" He lifted his gaze. Heartbreak in the dark brown eyes. "No one's seen Terry this morning. He was gone before sunup, before we got the call about Owen. Jeff stepped in and handled assignments this morning. Didn't tell me because he didn't want to worry me."

Something cold and foreboding settled in Duncan's gut.

"It can't be Terry, Duncan." Dad's head fell into his hands. "It has to be a mistake."

But Duncan knew Dad didn't actually believe that any more than Duncan himself did. "We'll figure it out," he muttered to his dad. He pulled out his phone and dialed Rosalie.

She didn't answer. If she was talking to the detectives, she might ignore the phone. So he didn't let himself worry. He just texted her. Call me. Emergency.

The text went unread.

She was just ignoring him. He wanted to believe that. Had to hold on to that possibility. It was the only thing that made sense. He knew that.

But he also had to act.

"I'm going to call the detective and give him this information," Duncan told his father. "And you're going to stay right here and rest for a minute, okay?"

Dad nodded without arguing, another terrifying turn of events. Duncan strode out onto his porch, not wanting him to hear this.

Heartbeat slamming into overdrive, he called the Bent County Sheriff's Department and jammed in the number for Detective Beckett's extension.

"Beckett," the man answered.

"Detective, it's Duncan Kirk."

"Great," he muttered. "What do you want?"

"Is Rosalie there?"

"I'm not an answering service, Kirk. You want to talk to your girlfriend, call her."

"She's not answering. And last I heard she was on her way to talk to you—"

"Me?" There was a slight hesitation. "You sure about that? Because I haven't seen or heard from Rosalie today."

That cold ball of ice in Duncan's gut turned into a full-on glacier. "What?"

"Do I need to repeat myself? Look, I'm busy, I—"

"I talked to her thirty minutes ago. She was leaving the hospital, and she was heading over to the sheriff's department to talk to you."

"Maybe she got sidetracked. Maybe she lied. Listen—"

"No, I need you to listen." Duncan took time for one careful breath, then laid everything out. Terry having the window of time to place that map. Terry not being on the ranch today. Everything pointing to Terry, Terry, Terry.

When he was done, the detective was silent so long Duncan was worried he'd lost the connection.

"Were you or your father aware that Mr. Boothe has been quietly buying up small sections of land in Idaho under an LLC?" Detective Beckett asked in that cop voice devoid of any emotion, even his usual irritation.

Duncan didn't fully understand the question, the information, but if they were looking into Terry… He just had to answer the questions and then this could all be over. "No. I wasn't, I can ask my dad but… No, I think he'd have mentioned it if he'd known."

"It also appears he's been stockpiling weapons—legally,

in fairness—and storing them on this property. We haven't been able to get a search warrant yet since it's across state lines, but since the weapons confiscated from your parents' house don't match the murder weapon, we're trying."

Duncan felt like his foundation was crumbling. "You think he did it."

"It's a lead we're following, and your added information is helpful. It should put some weight behind the search warrant."

Which was essentially a "yes, we think he did it." But... "What about Rosalie?"

"She might be driving. She might be at her office or following a lead. What do you want me to do? She's a grown woman. I can't go searching for her when I've got a murder to solve."

"Fine. Don't do anything," Duncan muttered, and he hit End on his phone. "I'll do it."

He was in his truck before he'd shoved the phone into his pocket. And he was out on the highway in under a minute.

ROSALIE RAN.

She'd managed to unbuckle herself, kick open the door of her truck, and then crawl out of it. The pain didn't register at first. She was moving on adrenaline and the desperate need to get away from Terry and his gun.

She didn't look back at the wreck of her car. Didn't worry about seeing how long it would take him to crawl out of the wreck. She had to get out of gun range, then she could worry about all that.

She knew where she was, and the closest safe place to run would be toward Bent and the sheriff's department. The ranches were too far away and so was the hospital.

Oh, she was miles from Bent, and it'd be a miracle if

she reached it considering there was a wet sticky substance dripping down her face. She didn't allow herself to think of it as blood. Acknowledging just how hurt she was would only slow her down.

She risked a look back toward the truck as she ran. She could see Terry crawling out of the back door. So she turned her attention forward and focused on running.

She had to get off the side of the road, even though someone might see her there and that might be help. It was too big of a risk considering how little traffic existed on this road. She needed to get out of Terry's line of sight. Or at least out of the range of his gun.

She pawed at her hip as she ran toward a cluster of trees. Her gun wasn't there. She'd lost it somewhere along the way. In the crash or the scramble out of the truck.

"Stupid," she muttered to herself. Careless. *Panic*. She knew better than to panic, but that's what she'd done. She cursed herself some more, but did it inwardly, so she could save all her breath for the run.

Once she was in the shade of the trees, she tried to get a better sense of her surroundings. She couldn't run much more. Her vision seemed to be getting…fuzzy, and not just from the sticky substance that kept leaking into her left eye. She was unsteady. Much more running and she'd fall and really hurt herself.

She leaned against a tree with both hands as she tried to catch her breath, tried to think through the whirling, nauseating chaos in her head. Pounding, pounding pain. By ducking the gun's aim when she'd crashed, the dashboard had given her a hell of a knock to the head.

But she wasn't shot, was she?

Luckily, her legs seemed to be holding her up. She just had to catch her breath and come up with a plan. She twisted so now it was her back leaning against the tree. She blinked her eyes a few times until she could see straight. Sort of.

She was in a copse of trees, probably planted by some long-dead pioneer. It gave her some cover, but no doubt if Terry thought she was hiding, this was what he'd go for.

She couldn't stay here. Not without a weapon. Not without her damn cell phone, which she'd left in the console of the truck.

But that wasn't too big of a mistake. If someone was smart enough to trace it, they'd find her truck crashed in that ditch. They could hopefully track her.

If Terry didn't first.

If worse came to worse and she was the next victim, surely some of Terry's prints or DNA would be in her truck. They'd find him. Justice would be served.

She tried to find some comfort in that, but was that all she wanted? *Justice?*

She thought about what this would do to Audra. Franny. Vi. The people who loved her.

Duncan. And maybe love wasn't in that equation. Too early, too soon for all that, but in this moment, Rosalie could be honest with herself, as little as she liked to be. It was somewhere in there, like a seed planted. Possibilities in all the things that brought them together, tied them together, made them *like* each other.

And sure, that was scary, but in *this* moment, the scarier thing was not getting a chance to see all that through.

So *hell no* she didn't just want justice. She wanted to live. She was going to have to fight. Creatively, sure, but fight nonetheless.

She hadn't paid close enough attention to how far she'd run off the highway route, but it couldn't have been more than a mile or two. Which meant she was smack-dab in the middle of nowhere on foot. The closest hint of civilization she could think of would be Hope Town—the former ghost town turned into a kind of community as a safe haven for people who needed it. But that still had to be miles off.

She could walk miles. She had concerns about the head injury, but she could walk miles. If she was slow and careful. If she kept to cover, like these trees. She could get there and then she could call the cops.

Something too close to panic bubbled in her chest.

But she couldn't panic. She had to think. Get out of the trees. Find new cover. Maybe if she could lure Terry deep enough away from the highway, she could double back and get back to the highway.

She pushed off the tree, had to close her eyes for a minute and breathe through the dizziness that threatened to take her out. She wouldn't let it.

She damn well wouldn't let anyone take her out.

Chapter Nineteen

Duncan sped his way toward Bent. His mind was racing in a million different directions. But he knew how to handle that, he reminded himself. He knew a million ways to focus. Back then, every game had felt like life or death.

Now that his situation *really* felt like life or death, he realized how ridiculous it had been to put so much pressure on himself for a *game*.

He gripped the steering wheel as hard as he could, especially with his bad arm, and focused on the throbbing pain in his shoulder. Sometimes pain could be a great focal point and motivator. He used it.

He drove with the idea he'd retrace Rosalie's steps. Drive to the hospital, then from there head to the sheriff's department. And if there was no sign of her, then to Wilde and Fool's Gold. And if she wasn't there, and hadn't gotten back to him, then what?

No. He couldn't deal in *then whats*. One step at a time. He made it to the hospital parking lot and finally had to force himself to loosen his grip on the wheel. He was sweating, a mix of worry and pain, and he needed to be more in control.

He did a quick circuit of the hospital parking lot. He

saw his mother's car. Wondered how Owen was doing. He should stop in, make sure Mom was taking care of herself.

He would. He'd come back. Once he figured out what the hell was going on with Rosalie. It was probably something so ridiculous, and yet he couldn't get past this driving need to make *sure*.

Because maybe she was just ignoring him, but it didn't *feel* right. She'd said she would call him, and she'd said so reluctantly. Rosalie might want to push him away sometimes, but she wasn't a *liar*.

But she could have gotten caught up in something, and then wouldn't he feel stupid if he'd gone around tracing her steps?

"I'd rather feel stupid than guilty," he muttered to himself, driving back out of the parking lot of the hospital. He got back on the highway that would lead him to Bent and the sheriff's department.

He was so intent on getting there, he almost missed it. A glint of something on the side of the road. He didn't even fully mean to look into his rearview mirror to see what it was. But when he did, he slammed on the brakes. With his breath caught in his throat, he pulled an immediate and very illegal U-turn, going down the highway on the wrong side so he could pull up on the shoulder that allowed him the perfect view of a truck crashed into the ditch.

With a buzzing in his ears and his entire body feeling completely numb, he shoved the truck into Park, jumped out, and ran over to the crashed truck.

Rosalie's crashed truck.

The driver's-side door and back-seat door were open and when Duncan ran around the full length of it, he realized it was empty. Empty was good.

Right?

He let out a pained breath, then started a closer inspection of the car on the driver's side. He noted her phone was in the console, which wasn't...right. It couldn't be right. He didn't see anything else out of place or strange, except when he stepped away and realized the little smudge on the driver's-side door's window looked a lot like...blood.

He didn't let himself think about that, because there was no one *here*. Which meant if she'd had an accident, she'd gotten out. No one was dead here, and that was what mattered.

But why wouldn't she be here? Why wouldn't she have used her phone to call for help? It didn't add up and Duncan didn't know what to *do*. Where to even begin. She had to be around here somewhere. Bleeding. Maybe she'd tried to walk along the side of the road?

But why would she leave her phone?

Since he didn't have the first clue, and his gaze kept getting pulled back to the *blood* on the window, Duncan knew he needed help. He thought about what Rosalie had done when his place had been trashed—she'd called Detective Beckett directly on his cell.

A number Beckett had handed out to his parents that first night, and Duncan had the good sense to have added to his contacts. He dialed it now.

"Beckett," the man greeted tersely.

"It's Duncan—" Before he could even get his last name out, Beckett was cursing.

"If you call me again, I'm—"

There was no time for that. "I found Rosalie's truck crashed in a ditch on Route Two. She's nowhere to be found, but there's some blood."

For a moment, the detective said nothing. "Where on Route Two?"

Duncan looked around, tried to discern what mile marker he'd be at. Gave the detective an approximation.

"All right. You're going to stay put. Right by the truck. I'm going to send an ambulance, then I'll be out. Once I get there, you're going to get the hell out of our way."

Duncan knew Detective Beckett was right. The police knew what they were doing. Detectives knew what they were doing. But he couldn't bring himself to verbally agree.

"Listen. This is dangerous. Terry Boothe's truck was found parked in an abandoned garage not far from the hospital. There's a threat here. I'm on my way. You need to step back and let the police handle it."

Duncan considered it. For maybe two seconds. Terry had left his truck near the hospital? Where Rosalie had last been?

No.

"Sorry. Can't do that." He hung up. Surveyed the quiet world around him. What had happened here? An accident? A fight? She hadn't *just* crashed, or she'd still be here. She would have used that phone to call it in or at least taken it with her.

Something bad had happened. Maybe it wasn't Terry, but too much was adding up.

Duncan took a few steps away from the truck in the tall grass. He could kind of see where some of the blades had been depressed by someone stepping on them. He'd follow the trail as best he could.

But before he could take even two steps, his toe hit something hard. He looked down and saw the glint of metal. He crouched to examine it. He couldn't be sure it was Rosalie's, but it was definitely a gun. So he picked it up.

He had a bad feeling they were going to need it.

ROSALIE STUMBLED, her stomach roiling so much she thought for sure there was no way she'd breathe through the need to wretch.

But she managed. On her hands and knees, the muddy ground seeping into both, she managed to swallow down the need to be sick. She blinked at the gunk in her eyes, but she couldn't see. She wanted to believe it was just blood, but she knew better.

She was losing consciousness. The grip of black was edging around her brain, and she kept fighting it off, but only barely.

"Come on," she muttered to herself. "Get it together." She sucked in a deep, painful breath, then pushed off her arms so that she was upright on her knees.

But the sight that greeted her wasn't a good one. Terry was approaching. He'd caught up with her. Found her.

Now what?

She tried to get to her feet, but her legs wouldn't seem to move, so she tried to scoot back, away from him. She groped around on the ground for something, anything she could use as a weapon.

"You've made this much harder than it needed to be, Rosalie," Terry said, walking in slow, menacing steps toward her. "I could have buried you out here. It could have been easy, but you had to wreck that truck. Now, we've got to complicate things."

He moved toward her, and she tried to scramble away, but she couldn't seem to get to her feet. She just stumbled, and then she felt his hand on her arm and she was being dragged back. She *thought* she was kicking. She was trying to kick, but it didn't seem to change the steady slide of her body across the ground.

"You left a pretty nice blood trail. Now, do we think

it'll be the cops or Duncan who comes to rescue you? My money's on our boy. If not, that'll be okay. It can still look like him. It'll look like him."

She tried to speak, tried to get her mouth to move, but it wouldn't.

"You shouldn't have crashed the truck, Rosalie. You shouldn't have done it. But you did, so we'll deal with it."

She tried to push him away, but she had such little strength left. He had one arm behind her, then the other, and shoved her back against the tree as something wrapped around her. A rope?

She tried to focus on breathing over panic. Understanding what Terry was saying over wanting to start sobbing.

"You can't really think you're going to get away with this," she rasped.

"Of course I am. I have a plan. You've been ten steps behind it this whole time. So I've got time. To perfect it. To make it right. You shouldn't have brought Duncan into it."

Duncan thought she was with the police, but how much time had passed? Would he be worried? Would he tell them to look for Terry? Would anyone find her wrecked truck?

They had to. If someone started looking for her, they'd have to find it. If she could just stay alive…

"Why?" she asked Terry, though she wasn't even sure what she was questioning. Just this whole damn horror.

"Why." He snorted. "Ten years of planning thwarted by some uppity kid who'd never seen a day of hard work in his whole sorry life? No. It wasn't happening. It's *not* happening. I never meant to kill him. If he hadn't gotten messed up in the cows, hadn't tried to blackmail me, they'd be mine and I'd be gone. But now? Now I'll kill whoever the hell gets in my way. Him. Owen. You. Duncan. It'll end there. I'll be out of here once you two are taken care of."

The cows. Somehow this had all been about the cows? She couldn't think it through clearly, but that was secondary right now. Because right now she had to save herself. Save Duncan.

There had to be some way out of this mess, but she was having a hard time keeping her eyes open. A hard time making sense of her scrambled thoughts and the gray mist over everything. Her head bobbed forward, the world black again. Then she felt a sharp, teeth-rattling sting against her cheek. Her eyes popped open, and she realized he'd slapped her.

"None of that," he growled.

Her cheek throbbed where he'd made impact.

"We need you awake. This isn't going to fall on me."

She used what little strength she had left to spit—a mix of blood and saliva—right at his face.

He reared back his arm, so she squeezed her eyes shut and braced herself for impact, for pain, for the awful, awful consequences.

But nothing happened. She opened her eyes to the foggy gray and saw him, still standing above her, but he'd dropped his arm and taken a step back.

"Not yet," he muttered to himself, whirling around and stalking away as he wiped his face on his sleeve. "Gotta make it right, so not yet."

Every "not yet" gave her a chance. That's what she told herself.

No matter how dire it all looked.

Chapter Twenty

Duncan was no expert tracker, but he managed to follow boot prints and drops of blood when there was no grass and only dirt. Away from the road, toward the trees.

Why would she do that? He made it into the grouping of trees. Pine needles littered the muddy ground below. Boot prints squelched into the mud. Was he ruining them? He tried to walk around them in case more help came.

He made it to one side, noted a tree that looked like it had been walked around quite a bit. He crouched, wondering if he studied the markings in the muddy ground, he'd be able to have an idea of what happened. But next to a tree, on an upturned curved leaf, was a tiny puddle of something dark, and a few more leaves around the area had the same.

Blood. It had to be blood. Way too much of it. His heart twisted into a pained pretzel. What was she doing? Heading away from help like this?

He shook his head. Answers didn't matter. He had to find her. So he searched the area for where the footprints came out on the other side. The terrain was pretty open here, and it was hard to note where any footprints were back in the tall grasses.

But in the distance, he saw another cluster of trees. If she had run away from the road and toward the cover of the first group of trees, then left this area, wouldn't she likely run for more cover?

He heard sirens in the distance. Maybe he should go back. The cops would know how to track. They'd have a better way of dealing with this, probably.

But he was already *out* here. She might be close, and if that was *her* blood, how could he possibly turn away? He surveyed the world around him again. The trees were the only place to go. Since there was no way of determining tracks, he decided to follow his intuition.

He began to walk straight for it, cutting through tall grass and focusing on not tripping over a random boulder, hole, or God forbid, a snake. He gripped the gun in his hand, ready to use it if he had to. He knew how to shoot it, probably, though it had been years since he'd even attempted to use a gun and his shooting hand was somewhat compromised.

He wouldn't need it. It was just a precaution. Everything would be fine once he found her. Everything his dad had taught him as a kid would come back to him, like muscle memory.

If he even needed it. Which he wouldn't, he told himself, over and over again.

Every once in a while, he paused. Looked around. Listened. It wouldn't be smart to get lost, but...

He heard it in one of those moments. A kind of *snick* sound, far away, but followed by something like a grunt. It all sounded very...human.

He rushed forward toward it. Then forced himself to think, to slow down. He couldn't rush into potential danger without thinking things through, even if he hoped with all he was this was just a strange misunderstanding, not danger.

He thought he maybe saw shadows moving around in the trees. But he couldn't be sure. So he tried to keep a low profile, crouching down as he walked so he was hopefully hidden by grass if anything…bad was out there.

Or should he just rush forward? Guns blazing? She'd been hurt. Bleeding. Why was he being patient?

But something inside of him seemed to insist upon it. A cautiousness. Because this was all wrong, so it required… tact.

He couldn't really see through the grasses, but once he was close to the trees where he thought he'd heard things, he straightened a little so he could see.

Across the way, Rosalie was sitting down. He nearly rushed forward, called out, did everything wrong in the moment. But her head was kind of bowed, and he realized she was *tied* to that tree. She lifted her head a little, and he could see even from a distance that her face was a bloody mess.

Duncan's whole body went ice-cold. Then, worse, another body moved into his vision. And even though the man's back was to him, Duncan knew who it was.

Terry. A man Duncan had *trusted*. The fury, the disgust, roiled through him along with the utter terror that he had Rosalie *tied up* and a gun in his hand.

But Duncan couldn't think about betrayal right now. He couldn't think about his worry for Rosalie. He had to think about how he was going to get her out of this.

He had a gun, but so did Terry. Duncan could see it there glinting in the man's hand. He thought Terry was speaking, the faint grumble of words on the breeze, but Duncan couldn't make them out.

Should he get closer? He had to get closer. He could

hardly just crouch here hoping something magically worked out right. He had to get in there and somehow…

Hell, he was no cop, no white knight. The idea he should be the one to *save* her seemed ludicrous, but there was no one else to do it.

He gave the cluster of trees a wide berth, trying to move closer *slowly*, with the grasses providing cover and the breeze distorting any noises he might be making. He found himself with a profile view of both Terry and Rosalie, and he could actually make out the words Terry was saying.

"We can wait him out. We can wait him out." It was the kind of repetitive thing someone said to themselves to convince themselves of something that was becoming less and less true.

"Seems to me there's sirens in the distance, Ter," Rosalie said. She sounded…tired, but she'd managed to infuse the sentence with some of her usual sarcasm. Even as awful as her face looked, bloody and bruised.

He swallowed down everything. This wasn't all that different than taking the mound in a World Series game. Sure, it was life or death, but if he shoved that away, it was the same process. Block out the noise. Settle into your body. Focus.

He carefully lifted the gun, using his right arm to support the dominant left one. His shoulder ached and throbbed and *burned*, which couldn't be good, but he knew how to play through pain.

He tried to remember all the advice his dad had given him, but that gun had been different. Hell, Duncan had been different—a kid, essentially, when his dad had taught him how to do this. Still, it had to be done, so…

He curled his finger around the trigger, aimed at Terry,

and pulled. Swore at the jolt of sheer agony that went from shoulder to fingertip.

Duncan cursed his bad arm as the bullet hit a tree about two inches to Terry's right, and Terry whirled toward him, lifting his own gun.

He didn't shoot right away though. He aimed, Duncan aiming right back. He could hit his target this time. He would.

"You wouldn't shoot me, Duncan. You don't have it in you. And even if you did try again, you missed the first time."

"I won't this time," Duncan said, pulling the trigger after the word *won't*.

And he didn't miss—Terry jerked back, even as Terry's bullet whizzed past Duncan, far too close...but not close enough.

ROSALIE FIGURED SHE'D SCREAMED, and she didn't *think* she'd been hallucinating sirens, but who knew? Who knew?

Her teeth were chattering, and she could only barely make out what had happened with the second shot. Terry lay writhing on the ground. Duncan ran over to her.

He was saying things, but she couldn't quite make sense of them. She thought maybe he was trying to untie her.

"Well, I didn't have getting saved by a baseball player on my life bingo card." But he had. She really hadn't had a way out of this one. Tears threatened—not just emotion, but pain and relief and a million other things as her arms fell to her sides.

She couldn't really feel anything. A creeping numb feeling was overtaking her, but he'd untied her. And then she felt him lifting her to her feet. It took his grip on her arm and her leaning against the tree to manage to stay upright, but she was free and standing.

"I'm carrying you," he said.

She managed a huff of a laugh. "Hate to break it to you, but that bad arm's going to let you down there."

"Well, I'll just get another surgery. Come on."

She couldn't even seem to move her head to look at him, but she could see Terry. In front of her. Still moving. In fact…

She pawed at Duncan's arm. "Duncan, he's getting up."

Duncan shoved her behind him, and she wanted to shove him right back, but it was taking everything in her to stand on her own two feet.

Terry got to his knees. He was gripping his shoulder where blood was pouring out of the gunshot wound. He was white as a sheet, but he was getting up, and he still had a gun gripped in his hand. Luckily, the wound in his arm should keep him from getting a decent shot off, but still.

"Give me the gun," Rosalie ordered Duncan.

"Rosalie."

"I've got it, Ace. Give me the gun and hold me up. I'm a damn better shot."

"I should hope so. I haven't held a gun for over fifteen years," he muttered. "But you're covered in blood."

She didn't mention her vision wasn't all there, no more than her strength. "What are you going to do then?"

Duncan stood in front of her—a human shield she didn't want. Terry clearly was trying to raise the gun in his hand, but he couldn't because of the gunshot wound in his shoulder. Meanwhile, Duncan held his—*her*—gun pointed at Terry.

"Drop the gun, Terry. Just drop it."

"You couldn't shoot the broadside of a barn," Terry growled, but it was clear he couldn't aim his gun either.

"I don't know what happened, but you're not walking away from this. You're not hurting any more people. It's over."

"It's not over. It'll never be over." Terry's voice hitched. Despair and panic and something else Rosalie couldn't quite name. Maybe a mental break.

"I'm the victim here," he shouted, stumbling forward a little. He was sweating now, either from the pain, or the attempt to lift his arm.

"Victim? You're a murderer. You betrayed…everything my father did for you."

"Did *for* me? He *stole* everything from me." Terry stepped forward, eyes wild, shirt getting darker and darker as blood seeped out of his wound. "Norman Kirk always got everything. His parents bought my parents' ranch and I was left with nothing but a measly ranch-hand job. He married Natalie. Natalie was *mine*. I saw her first. She was always supposed to be mine."

"Holy hell," Rosalie muttered. This was deeper and more twisted than she could have imagined.

"I waited. I planned. I'll get mine now. I put in the work. I put in the damn work. It's all mine now. No matter what I have to do to get it."

"The police know Terry. About the land in Idaho. The stockpile. And I have a sneaking suspicion once they get the search warrant they're after, they'll find my father's missing cows."

Terry's entire face arrested in a kind of shocked horror that chilled Rosalie to the bone. She tried to reach out to take the gun from Duncan. If he wouldn't take Terry down, she would. Impaired vision and all.

"That'll be enough," a commanding voice interrupted. All eyes turned to Copeland stepping through the trees, gun drawn. There were a few other cops stepping into the shaded area as well, around Terry to make a circle. Detective Delaney-Carson. Sunrise's sheriff, Jack Hudson, and another Sunrise deputy.

"Drop it," Copeland instructed Terry. "Now."

Rosalie didn't know if she was the only one who saw it—the wild desperation. The choice in Terry's eyes. Give up or go down swinging. She didn't wait to see if anyone else would recognize it. She just kicked out, so both she and Duncan fell in a heap on the ground.

Just as Terry swung his bad arm up, aimed and shot.

Aside from the pain in her head, she seemed to be okay, and Duncan had only grunted a little as he'd landed on his bad shoulder, she figured in an attempt to keep his full weight from falling on her.

Duncan looked up, so Rosalie did too. She saw the point where the wood had splintered from the bullet—where they likely both would have been hit dead-on if she hadn't pulled him down. Then he looked down at her.

"Well, I guess we're even, Red," he said, and he didn't shake, but his voice was raspy.

"I guess we are," she replied, though things were going a little grayer as Duncan detangled himself from her and helped her into a sitting position.

The cops were wrestling cuffs onto Terry, talking into their radios.

"She needs an ambulance," Duncan shouted at them.

She did. She knew she did. But still, she could hear the worry in his voice, feel it in the way he gripped her. "I'm okay." She squeezed his forearm until he looked away from the cops and at her.

"You don't look it," he grumbled.

"No. Probably need a few stitches. But I'm going to be okay. It's all going to be okay." She had never been any good at comforting people. Tended to shy away from it, but she pulled him into a hug anyway. Held on. "We're all going to be okay."

She felt him sigh against her. His grip on her was gentle, probably worried he was going to hurt her. But he held her all the same.

Because she wasn't lying. Everything was going to be *okay*. She'd make sure of it.

Chapter Twenty-One

Duncan hadn't wanted to let Rosalie go, but the paramedics had jogged onto the scene—stretchers and bags in tow. They'd loaded up Terry first, which had ticked him off, but one of the paramedics checked out Rosalie, right there with her sitting against the tree.

She'd argued with the woman, but the paramedic had been adamant. She'd have to ride in the ambulance to the hospital. Duncan had been somewhat relieved at how bitterly Rosalie had been against it. She had to be feeling at least a *little* like herself to mount that argument, no matter how terrible she looked.

He wasn't allowed to ride with her, which was infuriating, but he also didn't want Detective Beckett or even Detective Delaney-Carson explaining everything to his parents. It needed to be someone who would understand what a betrayal this would be to everything his parents held dear.

For thirty-plus years they had trusted Terry. That was an entire lifetime of believing someone was your friend. Someone you could trust and believe in. To have Terry be a murderer…

He sighed as he took the stairs to his parents' house. Rosalie had told him to go handle this. He hadn't even needed to explain—she'd understood. Since the paramedic had assured him that she'd need stitches, maybe go through a concussion protocol, but she would be okay, he'd let them wheel her away.

He'd given his statement to Detective Beckett. Gotten the clear to return to his truck and go break the news to his parents.

So here he was. Handling it. Audra would meet Rosalie at the hospital, and it wasn't like they'd let him in the room while they patched her up. He'd head out there later. Once he was sure his parents were okay.

He tapped on the door, then let himself in. Mom and Dad were in the kitchen, and as he approached, Mom stood from the table. She crossed to him, wrapped her arms around him and squeezed.

Dad stood next to the table looking pale and frail but determined to take it. They knew it was Terry now, but they didn't know the why of it.

"Just lay it all out," Mom said, pulling back, but gripping his hand.

He gave Mom's hand a squeeze then led her back to the table. He sat down and laid it all out to them. Terry hiding in Rosalie's truck at the hospital. Rosalie wrecking her truck to get away.

Terry having his own land, a stockpile of weapons. Duncan even shared his theory about the missing cattle. He didn't want to explain Terry's reasoning, but he had to.

"Saw me first?" Mom laughed bitterly. "I never gave Terry Boothe the time of day." She leaned into Dad, more troubled than Duncan wanted to accept.

"All these years…" Dad trailed off, and never finished that sentence.

"The police are still collecting all the information," Duncan said. "Terry made it sound like he's been resentful and planning this since his parents sold their ranch to Grandma and Grandpa, but the evidence doesn't support it. Maybe he always felt that bitterness, but he didn't start acting on it until a few years ago."

He'd hoped that might ease *some* of the hurt written all over his parents' faces, but it didn't. But they gripped each other's hands, leaned on each other.

They asked a few more questions, but mostly it would just take…time, Duncan supposed. And it would probably never fully heal that wound, but they'd survive. They had each other. They had him.

And despite Terry's attempt to take out Owen again in his hospital room, the kid was fighting. If he made it, he'd be able to testify against Terry over what Terry had done to him.

Nothing erased what Terry did, particularly to Hunter, but there would be justice. Duncan would use all of his resources to make sure of it.

Mom reached her free hand across the table to put it over his. "How's Rosalie?"

"They're patching her up. Audra was going to text me when they're done."

"You should be at the hospital. You don't need to worry about us."

Duncan looked from his mother to his father. He worried about them, and there was no stopping it. This was devastating. But there was nothing Duncan could do to fix that, and *that* sat on his chest like a heavy weight.

Dad stood, cleared his throat. "I'm going to need to go tell the ranch hands before the rumors go wild."

"I can—"

Dad shook his head. "This is my responsibility, Duncan. You stay with your mother." He strode out of the room.

Duncan looked at Mom, who was watching Dad with worry in her eyes. But she closed them, inhaled and exhaled carefully.

"He'll be all right. It'll be all right. It'll just take some time to…smooth out. You should go see Rosalie. And while you're gone, I'll make her a cake. Some cookies. A feast."

Duncan laughed in spite of himself. It felt almost normal. Bad things happened, and Mom swooped into action and comforted with food. It felt good and right.

He figured he could leave her and she and Dad would just be fine. After all, they had each other. Always had.

Still, he pulled her into a hug, and he squeezed her tight, wanting to transfer some kind of certainty that everything from here on out would be okay. For a moment, she even let him.

Then she pulled back, patted his cheek. "We'll all be all right. No one gets through life without some hard times. Love is what gets us through."

Because the sheen of tears in her eyes twisted painfully in his heart, he tried to lighten the mood. "Is that a not-so-subtle hint, Mother?"

She smiled at him. "I love you, Duncan. And I'm very proud of the man you are, who'd rush into help and save others, even though it's not your job."

"Everything good I am is because of you and Dad. Everything."

A tear slipped over onto her cheek, so he pulled her into another hug. Yeah, life was hard. But no matter the hard, he always had them, and they had each other all these years.

They'd all be just fine.

ROSALIE FELT NAUSEOUS. They'd stitched her up, done annoying tests on her cognitive situation, then yapped at her incessantly about concussions.

They were keeping her overnight, just to be sure she hadn't done more damage than they could see at the moment. Which was annoying as all get out.

Almost as annoying as Audra flittering around the room trying to make it *comfortable*. Rosalie was glad when someone else came into the room, even if that someone else *was* Copeland Beckett.

"She's resting," Audra said primly, scowling at the detective.

To Copeland's credit, he *almost* looked sheepishly at Audra. "No more questions. Just an apology."

"An apology?" Rosalie said. "Come on in."

Copeland's mouth quirked as he moved closer to Rosalie's bed, clearly ignoring Audra's scowl.

"I could have told you we'd narrowed in on Terry Boothe," he said, almost sounding contrite. "That might have avoided today's events."

"*Should* have told me. *Would* have avoided." Except she wasn't so sure about that. Everyone had been working for answers, and sometimes there was just no one right way to find them. They'd worked together, and just happened to coalesce on the same point without enough time to avoid Terry's violence.

"I don't owe you details on an ongoing investigation," Copeland said irritably. "It's not my fault we were coming to the same conclusions at the same time."

Rosalie grinned at him, immensely cheered at his bad attitude. "I thought this was an apology."

Copeland grumbled something under his breath. "I am sorry you got caught up in this. But you handled yourself." He jerked his chin toward the bandage on her head. "You and your baseball player."

"Yeah, he saved the day. So did I. You…?"

"Arrived in the nick of time and arrested the guy? You're welcome."

She laughed, then winced a little when a dull pain sliced through her forehead. "All's well that ends well. Apology accepted. I plan to lord it over you every time we have to work together."

"I expect nothing else." He gave an uncharacteristic awkward wave, nodded at Audra, then strode for the door.

But the thing was, just as she'd told Duncan, she and Copeland were a little too much alike to get along. And too much alike not to understand each other.

"You're right. We all did what we could. No guilt, okay?"

He stopped at the door, looked back at her with an unreadable expression on his face. "I'm incapable of feeling guilt," he replied.

Of course that was a lie. He wouldn't have come here, apologized, without *guilt*. But she let him leave with that parting shot. Looked at her sister, who had a thoughtful expression on her face.

"You know, I'm fine. You don't have to be here."

"Don't be ridiculous, Rosalie," Audra said, her own brand of irritable. She pulled a chair next to the bed. "I think it's time to have a talk."

"Can it wait? I'm tired." And she was. Tired and feeling *gross*. She wanted tonight over with so she could go home tomorrow.

She refused to think about Duncan in this moment. Having to break the news to his parents, not just that Terry was a murderer, but that he had all that resentment for the Kirks all this time.

It made her heart clench, and she didn't want to deal with it.

"I'll let you sleep in just a minute. But for now, you're

stuck in this bed and Duncan saved your life, so you're going to have to finally listen to what I've been trying to tell you for days now."

Rosalie shifted uncomfortably. "Come on, Audra. I'm in pain," she said, hoping to appeal to her sister's usually soft heart.

But Audra's expression was firm, and that was the thing about Audra. She had a lot of soft spots, but once she decided something, it was *decided*.

"Well, this is going to be painful, so it's the perfect time. I can't have you taking another step of your life thinking that because you loved Dad, you can't trust your feelings. There's nothing wrong with your instincts."

"Hell, Audra, can we—"

But Audra plowed right over her protests. "It was me. Every thoughtful present he ever gave you, every phone call he made on your birthday if he wasn't home. Mom too. The both of them were selfish and self-obsessed. And I hated that for *me*, so I set about to do something about it for *you*. I made them give you, or faked them giving you, everything I wanted."

Rosalie could only stare at her sister, stunned into complete silence. She knew her sister was just that kind of selfless. But it had never occurred to her...

"Audra. Why...?" She shook her head, trying to blink back the tears. She couldn't.

"I love you. I wanted better for you. If I'd known that meant you thought you had some sort of warped radar when it came to people, I wouldn't have. I thought I was doing the right thing."

Rosalie couldn't breathe for a minute. It was so awful. So...painful. Because if Audra had done all that, it meant...

No one had ever done that for her. The thoughtfulness. The showing of care.

"You have always done the right thing," Rosalie rasped out.

Audra sniffled, blinking back tears. No doubt refusing to let them fall. "I hope that's true, but the only way you prove that to me is to realize Duncan is perfect for you. Natalie and I wouldn't have conspired to toss you two together at every opportunity if we didn't think so. And I shouldn't have to tell you that, because he saved your *life*."

"I saved his too," Rosalie said somewhat petulantly, because her heart felt big and bruised.

"Rosalie."

"You…" Rosalie couldn't decide if it was the head injury that felt like her brain was scrambled, or just these revelations.

The invitations. The Tupperware. She had been soundly and thoroughly *tricked* into being in Duncan's orbit.

She wanted to be offended, but a knock sounded on the hospital-room door and after a moment, Duncan stepped inside.

So tall and handsome and *good*. He *had* saved her life, even if she'd had the presence of mind to save his after. He'd done it first.

And all her life, Audra had been saving her heart. Stepping in to make her feel loved because their parents were incapable.

It felt…small and childish to keep thinking that all the ways Duncan was *perfect* for her, even if he wasn't perfect, wasn't good enough because of some internal, messed up thing on her end.

It would be betraying everything Audra had done for her.

"I guess I'll forgive you," she murmured to Audra.

"I should hope so. You owe me a hot, rich guy in return."

"I'll see what I can do." And she would. One way or another, she was going to find her sister exactly this. And better, she was going to be everything Audra had been to her growing up. She was going to step up in all the ways she hadn't for the people she loved.

She looked at Duncan as Audra got up, said a few words to him, then left them alone in the room.

He approached her bed. "Heya, Red."

"Heya, Ace." She wasn't going to blubber all over him. She *wasn't*. But it took some effort to blink back the tears. Especially when he bent over, tenderly brushed some hair out of her face, then gently pressed his mouth to hers. Just as easy as that.

And it was easy with him. It always had been. All the things that made him who he was just seemed to *fit*. Even though he'd saved her, he hadn't made her feel like…she'd somehow lost. He'd made it feel like a team effort.

Because it was and they were.

"Did you know your mother and my sister plotted to throw us together?" she asked, her voice tight.

His mouth curved. "I didn't know about Audra, but I had some suspicions about my mother. That a problem?"

She managed to shake her head, even though it hurt. "No. No problems here."

"Good," he replied, then kissed her again. Like this was just who they were now. Together. A team. A unit.

Because they were, and maybe that was a little scary, but it was mostly pretty amazing.

Epilogue

One month later

Duncan had never been so happy to be back home in his life. The trip to LA to deal with a charity obligation, check in with the shoulder specialist there, and tie up a few other loose ends had been an interminable four days.

He'd tried to convince Rosalie to come with him, but she'd been in the middle of a case. Someday—someday he'd get her out there. He'd take her anywhere she wanted to go.

It didn't bother him that he was head over heels in love with her. He sometimes worried that it would bother *her*, so he hadn't said that yet.

But she'd spent most nights at his cabin. She invited him to her family dinners with Audra, Franny, Hart, and his wife, and stepdaughter. She'd folded him into her life as much as he'd folded her into his.

And it felt right. Every day, it felt right to wake up with her in his bed. Giving him a hard time about something or another, worrying over his arm, which really was starting to heal. Specialist-approved and everything.

He still worried about his parents, but Mom had thrown herself into helping Owen. Dad had worked hard to find a replacement for Terry, and Duncan had helped. He took on more and more of the day-to-day ranching than he'd dreamed he would. But it was…enjoyable. Working side by side with Dad.

Especially knowing he didn't *have* to if they started to get on each other's nerves too much. There was an open job offer at the high school for coaching, and Duncan figured one of these days, he'd probably miss the game enough to take it.

But, with his baseball playing career done, the Kirk Ranch really was *home* now. And he was eager to be back. He pulled up to his cabin, and pushed the truck into Park, staring at Rosalie's own truck in the drive.

He didn't allow himself to picture it as it had been crashed into the ditch, though that still took some effort. Instead, he focused on the pleasant surprise. Though she often spent the night at his cabin, he hadn't expected to find her here before the end of her usual workday.

Pleased beyond telling, he hopped out of his truck and ignored his luggage in favor of going to find her.

She was in his kitchen.

"Are you…cooking?"

She looked up, a scowl on her face that smoothed out when she saw him. Which never failed to amaze him. He hadn't been looking for her, for this, but he had another stroke of amazing luck in his life to have found it.

"I tried. I failed. Appreciate the sentiment."

He crossed to her, just as she crossed to him. Meeting in the middle. She wrapped her arms around his neck as his came around her waist. She grinned up at him.

"How's the shoulder?"

"Doctor said exactly where it should be. So there, worrier."

"I never worry," she said, and she lifted to her toes and

pressed her mouth to his. A welcome-home kiss that was just what he'd needed. Four days in LA hadn't been terrible, but this was the only place he really wanted to be.

"I missed you," he murmured against her mouth.

"You were gone for four days," she replied, trying to wriggle away from him. He didn't let her.

"Yeah. Say it."

She tried to dim her smile, but she failed that too. "Does it count if you make me?"

"Say it, Red."

"I missed you too." She moved to kiss him again, but he held her off, studying her face. Maybe she wasn't ready.

But she damn well should be. And if she could admit she missed him over just four days, he figured she could take it.

"I love you, Rosalie."

She stilled in his arms. Her eyes immediately wary as she studied his face. But she didn't pull away. Didn't *look* away, so he didn't either. It took a few moments, but after a few careful breaths, she softened there against him.

"I love you too, Duncan."

Yeah, this was the best home he'd had yet.

* * * * *